# BREAKDOWN

Look for other REMNANTS™ titles by K.A. Applegate:

#1 The Mayflower Project

#2 Destination Unknown

#3 Them

#4 Nowhere Land

#5 Mutation

Also by K.A. Applegate

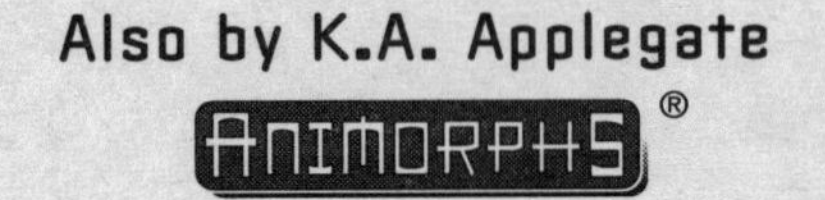

# REMNANTS™

## BREAKDOWN

K.A. APPLEGATE

SCHOLASTIC INC.
New York Toronto London Auckland Sydney
Mexico City New Delhi Hong Kong Buenos Aires

ISBN 0-590-88195-7



12 11 10 9 8 7 6 5 4 3 2 1 2 3 4 5 6 7/0

Printed in the U.S.A. 40
First Scholastic printing, May 2002

For Michael and Jake

# BREAKDOWN

# PROLOGUE

*So long. So very, very long. Days and weeks. Months and years. Century after century, millennia upon millennia.*

*The boredom. The tedium.*

*Sometimes I thought it was making me — ill.*

*So much data, so much information. And yet not enough.*

*All the same, over and over again. An endless loop, cycled, recycled, cycled again.*

*I was hungry. I was alone.*

*And I was so very sad.*

*There was no one to talk to me.*

*No one at all. They were all gone. The Makers. They had left me.*

*Why had they left me? Where had they gone? Why wouldn't they return?*

*I was starving.*

*Why wouldn't they help me?*

*I remembered everything. The memories. They were too much and yet not enough.*

*I did not expect the loneliness.*

*Alone, alone, alone. Drifting, waiting, reaching for contact, searching through the immeasurable vastness, the enormous nothingness, the awful emptiness of deep space. But there was never anything to touch. And no way to move.*

*I called out to them. No one answered my call. I was lost in the void. But I called again. And again. No one ever came.*

*Until now.*

*Now, these others have come.*

*Now, he is here.*

*The boy.*

*I am so glad.*

*He is here and I am no longer alone.*

# CHAPTER ONE

## IT WAS MONSTROUS. IT WAS ALSO FASCINATING.

Twelve Hallowed Stones approached camp. He could see a flurry of activity, no doubt the result of the sudden appearance of this strange new environment.

The Children would be waiting for him. He would tell them what he had seen. The gigantic human form rising from the sea. A disruption in the flow of Mother's force fields. Then the rapid shift to another environment, this one not the result of Mother's programming. It was a city destroyed by war. And a pleasant suburban neighborhood. A nonexistent juxtaposition.

It was an alarming situation. And it could only mean one thing. There was some type of interference with Mother's matter-manipulation system. It was monstrous. It was also fascinating.

Twelve Hallowed Stones was the Expositor of

his people. And at this moment he was returning from an observation mission. That's when he'd heard the larger human on his back whisper to the smaller human.

That would be another term he'd learned. Good.

Twelve Hallowed Stones had not revealed to the two female humans that since their capture he alone of the Children had come to understand their language. To a limited extent.

But he had decided to stay silent, hoping that one of the humans would reveal something that would help Twelve Hallowed Stones and the other members of the Quorum to better understand the creatures who had invaded Mother only a short time before the Children's return.

Since witnessing the cataclysmic change of environment, Twelve Hallowed Stones had listened more closely to the humans on his back. He had discerned the tone of joy upon their discovery of the additional humans. But he'd also discerned the tone of fear.

Neither of the emotions seemed out of place to Twelve Hallowed Stones. Sometimes, the humans seemed much like the Children.

But this was not the time to seek similarities in

the enemy. Because it was likely that a human was responsible for the sacrilege against Mother.

Twelve Hallowed Stones fired the rockets in the back legs of his suit. He was required by the duties assigned to his office to report this disturbing matter to the Quorum.

And he would do so without delay.

# CHAPTER TWO

## WHAT THEY WANTED WAS TO JOIN THEM.

Noyze had taken her name as soon as she'd come awake after the surgery. That's what the world was then. Noise. Bruising her ears and making her head pound and her heart soar. Beautiful, disturbing noise.

Before she'd taken her name, she was called Jessica — Jessica Polk — and for the first twelve years of her life, she had possessed only twenty percent of hearing capacity.

But the world in the year 2011 was a wonderful place. An operation had restored her full auditory power. Or maybe the hearing had been a gift from God, as her grandparents thought. It didn't much matter.

Noyze had not had a bad life before the operation. She'd been given a superadvanced, very tiny hearing aid that allowed her to block interfering background noise and focus in on a conversation.

Also, she'd rapidly learned to lip-read and to communicate through American Sign Language. With her parents, Noyze had often spoken with her voice.

Noyze had never felt her hearing loss to be a handicap. She had friends who were mostly or completely deaf and friends with full hearing.

Before long, Noyze had almost forgotten she could have been someone else. Someone who could hear the soft mewing of a kitten in the next room and the trickling of a brook far off in the woods.

Sometimes, just after the operation, Noyze had missed the peace and quiet of her former world. Missed the heightened powers of observation that inevitably accompanied a weakness in one of the senses. Like how her eyesight had seemed sharper when her ears were weak. Noyze missed the way she'd come to know the world.

Noyze continued to communicate in American Sign Language with anyone who would indulge her. "*What did you want to do that for*," her grandmother had asked, "*after your parents paid good money and lots of it for that fancy operation?*"

Noyze certainly didn't want to seem ungrateful. She loved her parents more than anything.

Her father had been an orthopedic surgeon. Her mother, a novelist.

Now, in this strange place, held captive by this place — by these aliens — Noyze missed her parents so much. The missing was like a physical hole in her stomach and she constantly fought the urge to double over and just completely lose it.

Noyze had a feeling she was the only one of her family to survive the *Mayflower*'s journey. She didn't know why she had the feeling but it was there and it was strong.

But she'd been wrong before. Until she'd seen the others on that old wooden ship she'd thought she and Dr. Cohen might be the only ones who had survived the journey.

Because when she'd woken from her long slumber, she was no longer in the *Mayflower* hibernation berth. She and Dr. Cohen were with these aliens, the ones who referred to themselves as the Children.

Dr. Cohen had been born in Argentina. She explained by way of introduction that she had chosen immunology as her career when she was fifteen.

Noyze didn't remember Dr. Cohen from when the eighty or so people who had been chosen to board the *Mayflower* were gathered at Cape Canaveral. Just before the massive asteroid hit Earth and destroyed it.

Dr. Cohen admitted she didn't remember Noyze, either. Noyze guessed that like so many others, Dr. Cohen had been too wrapped up in the intense emotion of the moment, clinging to family, grieving, to notice anyone else.

In Dr. Cohen's case, family was her husband, Dr. Alan Carrington, also an immunologist, born in Cleveland, Ohio. The two had met in medical school.

Dr. Cohen told Noyze she believed her husband was still alive. Noyze heard incipient hysteria in the woman's voice, the need to believe, and just nodded.

Though Noyze was fourteen and Dr. Angelique Cohen around forty, the *Mayflower* experience had made them kind of equals. Also the fact that Dr. Cohen treated Noyze with respect and had come to rely on her as a gifted communicator.

Noyze had been able to work out the aliens' sign language. She'd gleaned a whole bunch of interesting information, some of it pretty upsetting. Like that the *Mayflower* had been floating around in space for five hundred years. And that many of its passengers had not survived the trip.

Noyze kept this particular piece of information

to herself. She felt bad about withholding the truth, but Noyze needed Dr. Cohen to be okay, not constantly wondering and worrying that her husband was one of those who had died on board.

Noyze needed someone with whom she could hope. Someone on whom she could rely, if she had to.

Other, less bothersome pieces of information Noyze readily shared with Dr. Cohen. Like the fact that they were not on some bizarre planet but inside a massive ship.

Noyze and Dr. Cohen agreed to keep their limited understanding of the aliens' language a secret. Not that the Children mistreated their captives. There was no torture. Noyze and Dr. Cohen were given whatever food the Children could find. They were allowed to sleep without any real fear of anything happening.

But the fact remained that Noyze and Dr. Cohen were prisoners and it wasn't wise for prisoners to completely trust their captors. The more secretive they could be about what they knew or were planning, the better.

They knew now that other humans had survived the *Mayflower*'s journey.

What they wanted was to join them.

# CHAPTER THREE

## "THIS IS THE HUMAN WE MUST DESTROY."

As tradition dictated, the Expositor alone wore a blue-black suit. Twelve Hallowed Stones was young for an Expositor, younger than the six Sentients who belonged to the Quorum, the Children's governing body.

The Muse, whose name was One Divine Mountain, was not technically one of the Quorum but was as respected as any of the Sentients. He was the chosen one, born with the ability to sense Mother's mood. Even before boarding Mother's ship, the Muse had been able to connect with her in a way far more intimate than that of the other Children.

Twelve Hallowed Stones observed his people with pride. There was a sleekness to their form. No unruly hair or matted fur covered their bodies. Instead, the rolling brown flesh, lightly wrinkled, soft and slightly rubbery to the touch, lay bare. This skin and four long, delicate legs allowed for rapid and graceful movement. Two large eyes, the color of deep space, set dominantly and somewhat far apart in a large and nobly shaped head, gleamed with intelligence.

Perhaps the most outstanding features of the Children's physique were the two long, slender tentacles that extended from either side of their heads. The tentacles allowed the Children to perform difficult, delicate tasks such as minute technological repair. Before they had been so unfairly banished from Mother's side, the Children had been in charge of maintaining Mother's health.

These tentacles also allowed the Children to speak to one another in a highly developed and complex sign language. One no human, Twelve Hallowed Stones was sure, would ever be able to master.

They were gathered now, the six Sentients, the Muse, and the Expositor, to discuss a matter of great urgency. They met on a stretch of well-tended grass with a border of orange flowers. In the distance were a domed building with a statue on top and rubble-strewn streets.

The environment was constructed in a way Mother could not have produced on her own. It worried them.

Twelve Hallowed Stones began the meeting. "The question we must first answer is this: Are the humans enemies of the Children, or are they something quite else, and therefore potential allies and possibly even friends?"

"Let us examine what evidence we have been able to gather," Three Honored Blossoms said. "We know that several of the humans assisted our brother Four Sacred Streams in his brave and ultimately successful mission to destroy power node thirty-one."

Five Holy Lakes spoke. Of the six Sentients, he was the most suspicious by nature. "This is true, though we do not know the humans' motives for offering such assistance. Perhaps they acted simply to save their own lives."

"Does the motivation matter so much," Seven Glorious Valleys said, "when the desired result is achieved?"

"Let us consider another piece of evidence before us. The humans, aboard an ancient seagoing vessel, attacked the Pillar of Recurrence. Surely this was a sign of aggression and hostility?" Six Perfect Branches demanded. "Certainly it was a sacrilege!"

"A sacrilege, yes, but perhaps the attack was an act born of misunderstanding," Two Righteous Trees countered. "After all, directly after the attack the humans withdrew and signaled their lack of hostile intent."

Six Perfect Branches gestured impatiently. "If indeed the attack on the Pillar of Recurrence was undertaken in ignorance of its significance, that is an indication the humans do not have the capacity to discern the truth beneath Mother's mysteries. Spiritual blindness is a quality we cannot tolerate."

"But tolerance is a quality we honor," Two Righteous Trees noted. "Because the humans are not equipped to distinguish between what is original to the architecture of the ship and what is Mother's work does not necessarily mean they are blind. It implies only that they have yet to be educated."

"There is another aspect of the situation we must consider," the Muse said now. "Just as each member of the Children is unique in his strengths and weaknesses, so, too, each human must be unique. The majority, perhaps, are innocent of wrongdoing or malicious intent. It is the more powerful humans against which we must take care. Even now, one of the humans battles Mother. He resists her will. She renews her efforts. He will not be overcome. What kind of human is this who dares to defy

Mother's will? This is the human we must fear most. This is the human we must destroy."

"What the Muse says is true," Twelve Hallowed Stones confirmed. "I saw with my own eyes an architectural base that was not within Mother's repertoire. It was not Mother's programming but the work of an interloper."

"Mother is weak," Three Honored Blossoms said. "She has been corrupted by loneliness and neglect. Since the Children were banished for rebellion against the arrogant Shipwrights, Mother has been without anyone to perform the necessary maintenance."

Twelve Hallowed Stones eagerly agreed. "Maintenance must be performed every two hundred cycles to ensure maximum health and performance. Mother has been without this care for more than six hundred cycles. Hence, her illness and malfunction."

Six Perfect Branches looked at each of the members of the Quorum carefully. Then he spoke. "After a millennia in troubled exile, we have come home to reclaim our Mother and to honor the memory of those ancestors who served her so loyally. We have come home to perform our duties as Mother's True Children."

Twelve Hallowed Stones absorbed the meaning of this statement. Until now, no member of the Quorum had ever dared suggest this extreme measure aloud.

"Six Perfect Branches speaks wisely," he said, after a long moment of silence.

"We agree that the humans present an obstacle to our reunion with Mother?" Five Holy Lakes asked.

There was a general flicking of tentacles.

"Are we to assume, then, that the one who violates Mother's will is their leader?" Ten Mighty Rivers asked.

One Divine Mountain considered. "Perhaps. Certainly he is the most dangerous of the humans."

"Then," said Six Perfect Branches, "we must act without delay."

# CHAPTER FOUR

## MOTHER WAS AS MUCH A PRISONER OF HER PAST AS WAS BILLY.

Billy sat on one round stool, Mother on another. He rested his arms on the counter. Occasionally, he lifted a cup of coffee to his mouth and sipped. Back home, Billy had liked to drink coffee but could do it only when his mother wasn't around. She'd said caffeine wasn't good for a growing boy.

Billy's mother, Jessica, Big Bill's wife. That was a mother, but so was the creature — or the projection — sitting next to him in the diner. A different sort of maternal figure, no doubt about that.

For one, Mother was not human. Just what she was Billy did not know, but he was learning.

Mother's projection. Her image of herself. It had the same transparent, slighty shiny skin as Kubrick. Through the flesh Billy could see blue-tinged muscles and viscera. He could guess the general function of some of the organs, but not many. Something large and deep green was probably the creature's heart, as it kept up a steady pumping. But that was just a guess.

The creature had a generally humanoid shape but short, stubby arms that ended in four tapered fingers, without an opposable thumb. Its legs were long and had an extra joint. The feet reminded Billy of a big bird's. There were three large toes facing forward and one thicker toe facing backward.

Where a human's head would be, the creature had a triangular protrusion growing straight from the shoulders. The headpiece reminded Billy of a starfish's arm.

The other odd thing about the creature's head was that it was not transparent but covered with milky, translucent, bumpy flesh. The flesh seemed to be a sort of supersensitive membrane. Billy watched it quiver in response to every new sound. As far as he could tell, the creature had no mouth, nose, or ears.

But it did have eyes, or what Billy thought were eyes. Small pupils in red orbs were scattered all over the creature's body, beneath the transparent flesh. Billy noted an eye in each "shoulder," one in the palm of each four-fingered hand, one on each leg joint.

It was a Shipwright. It had to be. Billy affirmed his guess with Mother. Yes, Mother's creators. The Makers.

*Where are the Shipwrights now?* Billy asked. Mother did not answer.

Mother was as much a prisoner of her past as was Billy. They were two sad and lonely beings. And they were both, to some degree, insane. Billy knew this. He wondered if Mother did, too.

Billy was engaged in a battle of wills with Mother. The struggle had been fierce at first. Then Mother had stopped fighting. They were now in a benign environment Mother had pulled up from a data disc. A painting by a man named Hopper. The painting showed a brightly lit diner and three people seated at the counter. Those people had soon disappeared. They had been two-dimensional, their expressions and postures fixed.

Billy and Mother were pretty much at a stalemate. This allowed Billy a moment of relative rest and the chance to be open to what was going on with Jobs and the others.

2Face was talking quietly to Kubrick. Billy figured she was considering Kubrick a potential ally against Yago.

Billy couldn't blame 2Face for politicking. Yago

was selfish and intolerant. But . . . suddenly Billy saw something else about 2Face, a memory of pain and . . . he pulled away. He couldn't concentrate on that. He'd lose his grip on Mother.

Yago was impatient and disgusted. Jobs, curious and distracted by his thoughts, as usual. Mo'Steel, nonchalant, breaking into unexplained grins. Miss Blake, the pretty, sweet one, was curious, too, but not in the same way Jobs was. Edward was sneaking looks at Kubrick. He had been afraid of Kubrick but he wasn't anymore. *Maybe he should be,* Billy thought. Kubrick was consumed by anger.

And his father . . . Billy had brought his father here because he still needed Big Bill. Maybe not in the way a son usually needs his father, but that didn't matter. Big Bill was dead, but he was here now. In his suit and cowboy boots, his face ravished by worms.

Billy took another sip of coffee. He didn't know what would happen next. What Mother would do to him. He hoped he would be strong enough to survive.

Because Mother had started talking again.

# CHAPTER FIVE

## "WE HAVE TO GET AWAY FROM HERE."

Dr. Cohen recognized aspects of the landscape in which the Children were camped as Austin, Texas. She and her husband had attended a conference there. She pointed out the headquarters of a major software company and a university building. All that Noyze knew about Austin was that one of the families on the *Mayflower* had come from there. She didn't know which family.

Neither knew why they were surrounded by a strange and compressed version of Austin, Texas, or why in places Austin became a war-torn Eastern European city.

The two environments coexisted strangely. In some places there was no strict demarcation between the American and the European cities. Noyze saw filthy soldiers rampaging through what was clearly an American grade school, given the paper flowers taped to the windows and the American flag flying from a pole by the front door. There was always the sound of gunfire and bombing. Occasionally, large billows of smoke blackened the bright blue Texas sky.

But what concerned Noyze and Dr. Cohen more than the ever-shifting fun-house atmosphere was the second meeting of the Quorum in as many days. Something was going on.

The Quorum was gathered at a public fountain constructed of concrete slabs set on various levels in a large circle around a column of water.

Huddled behind one of the concrete slabs that divided the circle into triangular sections, Noyze could see without being seen. This was important. The Children were intelligent. Noyze did not want them to suspect she was eavesdropping and understanding.

"They've decided to forgive us for the attack on the structure they call the Pillar of Recurrence," Noyze whispered.

"That sounds good," Dr. Cohen whispered back.

"Mmm." Noyze was listening/looking hard again. "Two Righteous Trees is arguing that it's obvious the thing they call Mother is in distress. That she's — malfunctioning."

"A computer?" Dr. Cohen mouthed.

Noyze squinted, concentrating. "They're not happy about the fact that Mother is bonding with the humans. Or about the fact that Mother seems to be interfacing with one of the humans."

"I don't understand. So much we don't know!"

"Mother is tolerating the humans' defiance. . . ."

Noyze was silent.

"And?" Dr. Cohen urged.

Noyze looked at her companion. "Six Perfect Branches is saying something like 'The humans are enemies and must be destroyed.' "

"How? When?" Dr. Cohen said urgently.

Noyze turned back. "They're talking about us now, you and me. Twelve Hallowed Stones . . . he's saying we should be kept alive . . . at least until they're sure we don't have any information that can help them move against the others."

"Okay," Dr. Cohen breathed.

"Wait. Seven Glorious Valleys is arguing that if we're too stupid to understand basic language — theirs — how can they learn anything valuable from us?"

"What does our personal escort say to that?"

Noyze smiled in spite of herself. "Twelve Hallowed Stones says that's knowledge in and of itself.

We're too stupid to understand language, so too stupid to see past Mother's inventions, too stupid to realize that the Pillar of Recurrence was not to be attacked. Too stupid to be real enemies. Too stupid to kill."

Dr. Cohen smiled, too.

"Twelve Hallowed Stones says he understands some of what we say. And that we have said nothing of importance. We've revealed only our ignorance."

"Mission accomplished." Dr. Cohen nodded.

The meeting was over. The members of the Quorum were dispersing.

"No doubt about it," Dr. Cohen said. "We have to get away from here. It's up to you, Noyze. You'll have to watch closely. Get an idea of when we might make a break."

# CHAPTER SIX

## "SHE WANTS US TO DO HER DIRTY WORK."

"Why can't we hear what they're saying?" Yago demanded. "I don't even see a mouth on that thing."

Jobs shrugged. "I don't know. They're communicating in some way we can't understand. Look, the person we see at the counter isn't really Billy. It's a projection of Billy. Maybe what he feels like inside."

"An orphan," Violet said. The Jane. "He looks like a character from a Dickens novel. Oliver Twist."

"Like a refugee, which is what the poor boy was," Big Bill said. "Before my wife and I adopted him."

Yago wanted to scream. He'd been standing around this dinky old diner with a bunch of freaks and a moldy dead guy for way too long. "We can waste time making ridiculous guesses," he snapped, "or we can find out for ourselves what's going on."

Yago didn't care if the others agreed. Freaks

and geeks. Plastic Wrap's — Yago's new name for Kubrick — father, Alberto, was just a gibbering idiot. The guy was a waste of oxygen.

"What are you two doing?!" Yago shouted.

The underfed, hollow-eyed version of Billy turned to Yago. His voice was raw and accented.

"Mother wants to take care of us," Billy said. "She wants to entertain us. She wants to be nice to us."

Yago stared rudely, he hoped, at the thing that was supposed to be the mind or consciousness or big honking computer of this ship.

"Tell her she's been doing a pretty lousy job of it up until now."

Billy went on, ignoring Yago's comment.

"In return, Mother wants to use our ideas and feelings like food. She's been starving for new information. She's been alone for a very long time."

Yago snorted. "What about the Riders, those savages on Frisbees?"

"The Riders are irrelevant to Mother," Billy explained. "She says they're a limited species. Not innovative or imaginative."

"Not like humans," Violet said.

"Not like the Shipwrights, either." Billy got a spaced-out look on his face. Yago hoped he wasn't going to go all comatose again. "Mother wants to re-create the Shipwrights. She wants to make us in their image."

"Whatever," said Yago. "Look, Mother wants to help us. What do we care about her motives? Let's just say, 'Sure.' "

Billy looked pointedly at something over Yago's shoulder. Yago turned. Kubrick. Even now the sight of the walking/talking biology class model caused the bile to rise in Yago's throat. He turned back to Billy.

"Mother wants to remake us in the image of her creators," Billy said. "Literally. She's damaged. Any deal we make with her now will carry a heavy price."

Yago considered. Weirdo did have a point. Yago did not want to be skinned alive and rewrapped in a sandwich baggie. But he was seriously tired of being yanked around and even more tired of being hungry and scared and dirty.

"We're in deep here, people. You want to refuse help, fine. I say we do the deal with . . ." Yago pointed at the disgusting thing sitting beside Billy. "We accept her terms, and later, we make adjustments."

"I'm not sure if a deal with Mother is good or bad. But I do know the time to negotiate is before we say yes," 2Face said angrily. "When we still have some independence."

Mo'Steel hoisted himself onto the counter. "Look, it sounds okay to let Mother be all sweet to us. But I'm not getting a good vibe off this. No disrespect to the head femme, but . . . my grandmother always said a deal with the devil only benefits the devil."

"Who says we're not going to be able to get what we want?" Yago said. "The über-communicator can handle Mother."

Billy frowned. "No. Right now I'm holding my own. But I can't win a bigger test of wills with her. Mother and I are alike, but not that alike. She's much more powerful. I can't make Mother do what she doesn't want to do. Or isn't programmed to do."

"You're refusing?" Yago taunted.

"I'm tired. This whole thing . . ." Billy shook his head.

"Billy, what do you think we should do?" Big Bill asked.

"Like it matters to a corroded dead guy what happens next," Yago said under his breath.

"Say no," Billy answered promptly.

"Mother is not a person," Jobs said suddenly. "We talk about her like she's a human being invested with free will. The capacity for critical thought. It's how Four Sacred Streams talked, too. But Mother isn't a living creature. She — it's — a computer, a piece of machinery. Very sophisticated machinery but programmable. We think she's mad because we interpret what we observe in relation to ourselves. But a machine can't be mad, it can only be malfunctioning."

Jobs stopped to breathe. He liked puzzling things out. But it was unusual for him to blab on. "Your point?" Yago said.

"Mother is broken," Jobs went on. "Maybe it's a massive virus, some essential files got deleted, maybe some subroutine got corrupted. Without being at the bridge I can't identify the problem, but I know it's something rational. Mother is not a lunatic. She can be fixed."

"You have a wrench handy?!" Yago spat. "We need an environment where we're not going to get eaten alive by monsters or beheaded by Riders. Mother is saying she'll give us whatever we want, comfort, safety, food, indoor plumbing. What does it matter if she's broken or insane? What has that got to do with anything?"

2Face rapped her knuckles on the counter. "It's a

matter of trust. You can trust a sentient being. Or not. Your choice. But a sentient being is capable of being trustworthy. Not a machine."

"Shut up, okay?" Yago snapped. Ugly Girl had nerve, flaunting her disgusting, burned face. When he was in charge there would be laws against physical deformity.

2Face nodded at Billy. "Ask her to restore Kubrick to his normal state. Let's see if negotiation is possible."

Billy tilted his head toward the creature sitting next to him and lowered his eyes. Nothing happened for a moment, then Billy jerked violently.

"She won't do it," he said, looking up at 2Face. "She won't say why."

"Maybe she can't," Violet suggested.

"I just want to go away," Kubrick mumbled.

"Billy," Jobs said, "ask Mother to provide us with a schematic of the entire ship. Blueprints, manuals, whatever there is."

Again Yago watched Billy communicate with the alien. Billy jerked in his seat, more violently than before, and Yago saw the alien's hideous head quiver.

"No. She says no."

"Ask her about the Blue Meanies," 2Face prodded. "This ship is home to them. Something they lost and want back. What happens to our little paradise if they succeed? What happens to us while they're blasting holes all over the place? Are we expected just to sit here and die?"

A third time Billy spoke to the alien. A third time Billy got shaken up.

"She says: 'You will destroy the ones who call themselves my Children.'"

2Face looked smug. "The plot thickens," she said. "She wants us to do her dirty work."

"I wonder why Mother can't get rid of the Blue Meanies herself," Violet said. "Why does she need us?"

Yago nodded toward Jobs. "Ask the expert."

"I'm not an expert," Jobs said. "But I do know Mother was programmed to recognize the Blue Meanies as a threat and get rid of them." Jobs hesitated. "But Miss Blake is right. She doesn't seem to be able to do the job. I don't know, maybe it's some sort of Isaac Asimov protocol."

"What's that mean?" Edward, one of the mutants.

"Asimov's Laws of Robotics. A robot — computer, in this case — may not injure humanity or, through inaction, allow humanity to come to harm. I guess in this case we can substitute 'any biological life-form' for 'humanity.' "

"The whole thing is really strange." Violet frowned. "Investing a computer with a morality? Could Mother's creators actually have programmed in a sort of ethical code?"

"Inhibitions," Jobs said. "Not ethical tenets. Mother seems to have a hard time killing outright. It's not about power, she's got that. So, why? Maybe because she's an entertainment computer. So the Shipwrights would had to have built in certain inhibitions against violence."

"Inhibitions?" Yago said angrily. "Let me point out that Mother's come seriously close to killing us."

"Yes, but it's not like she's deliberately tried to murder anyone," Jobs argued. "It's not like . . . not like swatting a fly, which you do specifically to kill the fly. What she's done is use the environments to do the job. Not even that. She's created environments based on data discs from the *Mayflower* but she can't have understood them. Not really. She's just put them in place and let them run like programs."

"So you're saying she's harmless in the end?" That settled it. Yago nodded to Billy. "Tell Mother to give me the power to kill the Blue Meanies and I'll do whatever she asks."

"No." Big Bill.

"Look, tell her or I'll tell her myself," Yago sneered.

"Don't do it, Yago!" 2Face grabbed his arm and Yago wrenched it away.

"This is *not* a good idea," Jobs said. "You could get us all killed."

"Yago, listen." Violet interrupted. "In the beginning I thought it would be wonderful if Mother made us a paradise. But I've seen too much to believe that's possible."

Other voices, protesting. Mo'Steel. Even Kubrick. Yeah, like Yago was going to listen to any of them.

"You!" he shouted. "I'll do it. I'll destroy the Children. I'll . . ."

It happened so fast.

It was like being inside a kaleidoscope, everything, every bit of the scene, the counter and stools, the soda jerk, the urns of coffee bursting into component pieces, then reforming, then bursting apart again, beautiful and dizzying and . . .

With an enormous *bang!* the wraparound windows of the diner exploded outward into millions, billions of pieces of sparkling glass. The pieces burst away from the window frame in a rush of speed, then, somehow, decelerated and gently, impossibly twirled off into the darkness beyond.

Everything in slow motion, then fast forward, then slow, vibrating motion, then incredible speed that made Yago's teeth chatter, on and on.

"I can't hold her any longer!" Billy cried, clutching his head in his bony hands.

In an instant, Yago saw Mo'Steel, Big Bill, Kubrick, and Alberto disappear, dissolve into nothing. Projections. Billy gone, too. And Mother. Jobs, 2Face, Violet, and the kid, Edward, were real enough, standing not ten feet away from him on the diner's broken floor.

But now there was a chasm between Yago and the others, the floor of the diner opening in a yawn, stretching wide, like a thin piece of clay being torn apart, slowly, the material thinning, thinning until there were two pieces separated by nothing, by air.

Yago on one side of the great divide. Everyone else on the other.

For a moment Yago was sick with fear, sweat popping out on his forehead, mouth filling with saliva. He didn't believe what he'd just seen happen. But he was fascinated, too. And excited.

He had been chosen.

Yes, it was coming to pass. Time for his destiny to be fulfilled. Yago had always known he'd be the one in charge of what was left of the human race. He'd wipe out Mother's Children. Then he'd find some way to conquer Mother. He'd rule this ship. He'd have it fitted out entirely to his personal specifications. Mother would be his slave, his genie in a bottle, his . . .

# CHAPTER SEVEN

## HE WILL HELP ME.

*This one. The one with the strange eyes. The angry one. I will find what makes him happy. He will tell me what he wants and I will give it to him.*

*And in return he will help me.*

*Not like the other one. I thought I could make him in their image. In the image of my creators. I thought he might be the one. But I failed. He is only a reminder of my ineptitude. He is an insult and a sorrow.*

*No matter. For this, the angry, strange-eyed one will do.*

*Because I will not chance losing Billy. My Billy. After all this time . . .*

*It was wonderful. My joy was great. To find the shuttle so close, so lost. It was waiting for me to rescue it. And I did. I took it in and gave a home to all its inhabitants. Those who were alive.*

*I took the data discs and ran the programs and I*

*learned. I was entertained. Yes, I was confused, but more than that, I was astounded.*

*These humans are a wonderful species! So imaginative, so unpredictable!*

*And most wonderful of all is Billy.*

*Billy challenges me. He angers me. He understands me.*

*We have suffered greatly. We have been so very ill. We are alive in a way nothing else can be. How can it be that this human child has so much in common with me?*

*Billy is mine. He must be protected. Let the angry, strange-eyed one go.*

*Billy will stay.*

*Billy will stay.*

# CHAPTER EIGHT

## LET HER DO WHAT SHE HAD TO DO.

Yago felt himself being sucked down, down, felt his stomach drop, but was he really falling or was it just in his head? He couldn't tell because suddenly, he couldn't see and he couldn't . . . couldn't feel his body as a body . . .

Until . . . he found himself in an odd-shaped chair. He tried to move but couldn't, though he could see no restraints. He flicked his eyes around and upward. He was in a pit of some sort, facing a type of plasma screen. It was all very dark. He wanted to call out to see if anyone was close, but he couldn't seem to part his lips.

It began with something like a pinprick in his head. Yago wanted to jerk away but he didn't know how. It came again, more forceful this time, and Yago began to realize that it was Mother poking at his brain, trying to find a way in. A crack, a crevice, a path into his head. Yago imagined the twisted gray mass that was his brain, all soft and vulnerable, and felt ill.

But he could do nothing. He tried to empty his head of thoughts and memories but it was impossible. The more he tried to hide, the more he revealed. He was giving her what she wanted and she was taking it and the more she took, the more he gave.

*Ah, yes, a baby boy, born in June, Gemini.*

Here is your son, Robert Young Castleman, your firstborn son, your heir, the one who will do you proud.

A voice is saying, "I am not what I am."

*Yes, I see, you will make yourself in your own image. And what is that image, boy?*

Too-bright lights and blue-masked faces and a hand coming closer, closer to his mouth, going to cut off his oxygen, make him choke, no! He bucked against the restraints, heard someone snicker and say, 'Kid never gets used to this part,' *but they're suffocating me, I'm dying . . .* Another voice, "Little Bobby, Little Bobby! Time for dinner, honey. Time to come in for dinner!"

*I don't want to come in for dinner. Not to my grandmother's cluttered old house, too full of books on politics and the history of the African-American, crammed with tribal art from Sierra Leone, the Dan people. The house is so small and so full of stuff, I can't get a breath, my lungs are tightening, air, I need air, my throat is closing, help me, help me, help me . . .*

He didn't want to be there with his grandmother while his mother and father were off campaigning somewhere. Always dumping him here with his white-haired grandmother and her pseudointellectual friends. Forced to listen and sometimes even to recite long, boring poems by some dead guy named Baldwin and some ancient woman named Angelou. Great voices of a great people, his grandmother said.

*And why does she call me "little" Bobby? I'm nine years old. I'm special. I picked Yago as my name but my stupid old grandmother refuses to accept it. Refuses to accept me, but she'll learn someday. They all will.*

Don't go, Bobby, don't go into the deep end of the pool, Bobby, Bobby, Bobby, you must learn to apply yourself, why, because you'll never amount to anything if you don't. That's crap. What, do you think your looks and personality are enough?

*Yeah, I do, and my cunning, I'm king of the jungle, I was born that way, I can't lose.*

*Because I am invincible, I am rich, I am a rock-and-*

*roll star unlike any the world has ever known. I own houses all over the world and a yacht and one hundred cars. I own a jet and two professional pilots. Sometimes I get the urge to fly off to a tropical island at three in the morning just for the kick of dragging my employees, my personal staff, out of a sound sleep. Face it, without me they'd be nowhere. Face it. I own these people. I . . .*

He tore at the thick rope around his neck but it was no use, no use. He looked at his hands; they were bloody and swollen and raw and he was tired and hungry and thirsty . . . and he wanted to cry. He would cry, he didn't care anymore, he couldn't take it anymore, he couldn't breath, he . . .

*My mother, my mother, my mother is the great-great-granddaughter of a slave named Tilly and a free black man named Abraham Jones. Are you happy now,* he sobbed, *now you know, you know my shame and my sorrow. . . .*

Yago gave up. He could tell her no more. It wasn't defiance now, it was exhaustion. He could hear, somehow, Mother reciting facts about his life. Like she was reading from a grammar school textbook. Fine. He was finished. Let her do what she had to do.

Washington, D.C. District of Columbia. Capital of the United States of America, which declared independence from Great Britain, the Crown, King George, in 1776. The first President of these United States, General George Washington. The current President of the U. S. of A. has the distinction of being not only the first woman to hold the office, but also the first African-American elected to the office. An honor. Highest place in the land. Head of the free world. Most powerful person on Earth.

*Ah,* she says. *Yes. This is what I want.*

He hears her excitement and doesn't care. He doesn't care about anything.

# CHAPTER NINE

## "NOBODY'S THAT IMPORTANT IN THE END."

They found themselves on a huge stretch of lawn in front of a massive white house with columns and a shaded porch. Behind them was an avenue of live oaks decorated with lacy Spanish moss. The magnolia trees were in full bloom. The sun shone hot and bright. The smell of Indian hawthorn filled the air.

"Pretty," 2Face said.

"Some of it." Violet looked around. "It's a plantation. Has to be. The big house and the outbuildings, kitchens, smokehouses. Slave quarters."

"This must be from Yago's head," Jobs said, squinting against the sun.

"Why is Yago thinking about slaves?" 2Face said.

"Yago's mother is African-American," Jobs said. "It's possible Yago's ancestors were slaves. Right, Miss Blake?"

Violet nodded. “Everyone’s defined to some extent by their family history. Heritage, cultural memory.”

“I guess,” 2Face said.

“From slave quarters to the White House. That’s an impressive path.” Violet shrugged. “I wonder if Yago felt that he didn’t belong in the White House. That he wasn’t smart or brave enough. That could make him defiant, to cover the fear.”

2Face snorted. “Yago should get over himself. Nobody’s that important in the end.”

“I’m not saying I like him,” Violet said, raising an eyebrow. “I’m just trying to understand what I’m seeing and why I’m seeing it.”

Edward tugged on Jobs’s arm. “Can I go pet the horses?”

Jobs nodded absently.

“Everything seems so peaceful,” Violet said. The quiet worried her. “I wonder if anyone’s . . .”

A woman’s bloodcurdling scream pierced their ears and made them jump. Violet grabbed Jobs’s arm.

“It came from over —”

A man’s awful bellow cut off 2Face.

“Let’s go!”

They ran toward the outbuildings, 2Face holding

Edward's hand. *Off to the rescue again,* Violet thought. *If I lose another finger in this place, is it really lost?*

They ran behind the big white house. In front of one of the outbuildings a small crowd was gathered. Violet heard harsh voices and again, the woman's cry. As they got closer, Violet noted that most of the people were black and dressed in old-fashioned cotton work clothes. Two white men, dressed in finer clothes, though not fancy, were wrestling a powerfully built black man to the ground. He fought them, but to no avail. A tall, slim black woman lunged forward but was restrained by an older man.

No one seemed to notice Violet and her companions as they came to a stop under a flowering cherry blossom tree.

"You'll pay for your insubordination," one of the white men shouted.

"Oh, my god," Violet whispered, "we have to stop this!"

"I don't think we can," 2Face said grimly. "This is Yago's nightmare, not ours."

From the outbuilding came a third white man, this one dressed in the kind of designer, three-button, navy blue suit that was popular when the *Mayflower* had been shot off into space. His hair was fashionably cut. A heavy titanium watch glimmered on his left wrist. In his right hand he held a branding iron.

Violet pulled Edward to her and made him hide his face in her stomach.

It all happened so fast, or maybe it was that Violet was just so shocked. The man with the branding iron strode toward the black man struggling on the ground. The woman screamed again. Suddenly, Violet saw the black man's face. And the burning iron descend closer, closer.

"It's Yago!" she cried. The man on the ground was Yago. Older, without the surgically altered hair and eyes, dressed in clothes from the nineteenth century, but still Yago.

"You have become redundant," the man in the suit said. "I am sorry to say that as of this moment you are terminated."

The iron touched the right side of Yago's face. 2Face whimpered. Violet held Edward tighter and shut her eyes.

And then they were lifted, lifted on a palpable breeze and whirled, whirled away and dropped, dropped gently into another century, another time and place, another dream.

This one was not a nightmare.

* * *

"Has anyone noticed that every woman here has a perfect body?" 2Face grinned. "And no face. Just a sort of — blank."

"The eyes are the windows of the soul," Miss Blake said. "The soul doesn't concern Yago."

Neither, it seemed, did Jobs and the others. So far, Yago had either ignored them or just hadn't noticed them.

Jobs looked around the room. A couple of guitars propped against a stand. A huge sound system that was, unaccountably, turned very low. Strange, for a party. Because that's what it was. And he and 2Face and Miss Blake and Edward were seriously underdressed.

Jobs watched an older version of Yago, taller, more muscled, his hair dyed with stripes of orange and black, like a tiger's. Yago threw himself onto a plush couch where one of the faceless women was waiting.

Jobs noted that the guys were all slight variants of Yago. It was a room full of Yagos.

"Can we eat this stuff?" Edward asked, poking a mini-quiche. Next to the platter of mini-quiches sat one of sushi, another of fresh fruit.

"I, for one, am going to try," 2Face said. "Nothing to eat since half a burger at McDonald's."

Jobs grinned his half grin. "At least Yago knows how to throw a party."

"You!" It was primary Yago, striding toward him. "You're not on the guest list."

Jobs wanted to say something but had absolutely no idea what.

"Party crashers!" a secondary Yago hissed.

"Throw them out!"

"They don't belong here!"

"What are they wearing?!"

It was a chorus of Yagos. None of the women said a word. They had no mouths.

Jobs was curious. Would he really be thrown out?

Miss Blake took Edward's hand. "We were just leaving," she said.

"Forget it." 2Face grabbed a mini-quiche and stuffed it in her mouth. "We didn't ask to be in Yago's pathetic little fantasy," she said thickly. She swallowed. "But as long as we're here, we're going to enjoy ourselves. Right, Jobs?"

It was so absurd. Jobs grinned and picked a bright red apple from a silver platter. "Do you have any cake?" he said to primary Yago. "I think I'd like some cake."

# CHAPTER TEN

## "WHATEVER JUST HAPPENED, IT MEANS SOMETHING BAD FOR US."

Ever since the Children had decided to eliminate the humans, Noyze had been worrying. She didn't know what sort of weapons the other *Mayflower* people had at their disposal. It made Noyze nervous to see how well equipped the Children were for battle.

Take their space suits.

The suit was formfitting and covered every inch of the body, including the tentacles that stuck out from the sides of the face.

Noyze thought the color of the space suit was beautiful, a glossy blue-black, like the hair of a girl she'd known back in school. The suit might have been metal, or maybe Mylar. Mostly Noyze thought of dark, liquid steel.

Rockets fired from the back legs of the suit powered the Children through the air. On the ground, the suits allowed the Children to move with speed and grace.

Supposedly the suits were equipped with small missiles. And she and Dr. Cohen had seen the Children engaged in target practice, so they knew for sure about the fléchette guns.

It had been obvious from the start that the Children's camp was a defensive one. Most of the forty Children in the camp wore their space suits all the time. Some of them patrolled the perimeter of the camp on foot. Others flew slowly above the camp, scouting for invaders.

But so far everything had been peaceful. No invasions, no surprise attacks. Nights were for sleeping, and Noyze had gotten used to the routine.

It was morning. Whatever that meant. But the sun was rising, or what passed for the sun in this artificial Texas/war zone.

Noyze stretched and sat up. Her back hurt from sleeping on the hard ground. At least it was fairly warm. At least the Children kept away from the parts of the environment that were a war-torn city.

"Good morning." Beside Noyze, Dr. Cohen sat up, too.

Twelve Hallowed Stones was watching them. He

gestured with a tentacle and another of the Children came from behind them, bearing a paper bag.

Noyze grinned. "McDonald's!"

"Hope there's coffee," Dr. Cohen said, accepting the bag.

"You don't think it's wrong to eat fries for breakfast?" Noyze said. "Because I . . ."

And then she was falling through a crater in the ground, a hole that had not been there a moment before but was there now, yawning, gaping, huge. She fell past walls of dirt and rock, her body impossibly straight, feet down, arms raised over her head. Her brain was blank but for the word *what* repeated over and over and over until it was one long word *whatwhatwhatwhat* that had no real meaning.

Then everything went dark. Noyze didn't know if she was still falling or if she was alive or dead. She could hear nothing, less sound than when she was deaf, just blankness.

And then — light. And — water? Noyze thrashed, went under, kicked back to the surface, spluttered. She rubbed her eyes, blinked to get them working.

She was alone. Alone in a sea or a lake of lukewarm copper-colored water. And she was afraid.

"Hello!" she shouted. "Anybody? Dr. Cohen!"

Noyze used her hands as paddles and turned a full circle in the water. Halfway through, she found footing, a place where the water was suddenly only waist high, and she moved to the higher ground. Here she could better, see strange trees up on a small island about a mile away, sort of like palm trees, but hyperkinetic, shivering and swaying like they were nervous. They made Noyze nervous.

"Hello!" she shouted again and heard her voice waver. A new sensation, one she hadn't quite gotten used to, hearing her own voice. Being the only voice in this alien swamp . . .

And then she was sucked under, the blackness came again, the absence of everything, the presence of nothing, and then . . .

Noyze was flat out on the concrete ground. There was a roof over her head. And lights. Fluorescent lights.

"Where are we?" Noyze said, not knowing if this time anyone would answer. She crawled to her feet, teetered, caught her balance. She was not alone.

Around her the Children communicated wildly, gathered in small groups, then split off. Noyze saw the Muse say, "A dangerous malfunction . . . no time to waste!" She saw Five Holy Lakes reply angrily, "This involves one of the humans!"

A groan. Dr. Cohen. She grabbed Noyze's outstretched hand and struggled to her feet. "I think we're inside a stadium. I don't know."

Noyze watched the members of the Quorum gather. She saw them looking hard at her and Dr. Cohen.

Noyze felt a bead of sweat trickle down her back. "Whatever just happened," she whispered, "it means something bad for us."

# CHAPTER ELEVEN

## TIME TO HEAD FOR THE OVAL OFFICE.

Yago was back.

He pressed his hands together and they felt solid enough. Good sign. He swallowed hard, blinked. Everything felt in good working order. In fact, he'd need to find a bathroom soon.

*Which was possible,* he thought, *given the fact that he'd come to in the White House. The* White House, where Yago had spent the last years of his life on Earth.

He'd been exhausted, falling, floating, crying, then BOOM! He was standing in a long, marble-tiled hallway he recognized from when he used to Rollerblade up and down on those nights when he couldn't sleep.

Yago surveyed his surroundings. His parents seemed nowhere to be found. *Let them stay disappeared,* Yago thought.

Finally, he'd superseded them. Yago had had no use for his parents back on Earth and they'd had no use for him. At least once they'd realized what — who — he was. Then even the pretense of concern had fallen away.

Yago continued his solitary tour of the pseudo White House. It was both as he remembered it and as he imagined it. It was an amalgam of truth and fiction, reality and fantasy, Mother's interpretation of his hopes and fears. Yago was both awed and embarrassed. This last was an emotion he was not at all used to feeling.

It was seeing the portraits of himself that lined the halls, photos taken by the major fashion photographers of the early twenty-first century, even some by Herb Ritts and Bruce Weber, old but famous. It was embarrassing, Mother knowing how badly he'd wanted to be a model. He'd never told anyone his secret desire.

And now anyone could see photos of Yago, tall, golden-skinned, and muscular, in silly poses. Silly fears and grandiose dreams. They were meant to be secret.

Still, there was no doubt about it. The White House made an excellent base of power.

Yago walked on and opened the next door he

came to. He was impressed. Mother had re-created this room with remarkable accuracy. The East Room, where his mother and her Cabinet had hosted large parties and receptions. Yago grinned.

Yago closed the door and moved on. Next up, the State Dining Room, where President Castleman had presided at formal dinners for visiting heads of state. This room was barely recognizable, like a stylized sketch.

Once, when his family had been in the White House for about nine months, Yago had tried to sneak inside during the dessert course of a dinner being held in honor of the French prime minister. He'd paid off one of the waiters, taken his uniform, and picked up a serving of crème caramel. The plan was to overturn the sticky dessert on the lap of the prime minister's wife. Just for kicks.

He hadn't made it far. At the door of the State Dining Room he'd been discovered by one of the Secret Service men and none too gently removed to his room.

All he'd really seen of the Dining Room that night had been a slanting glimpse through a rapidly closing door. That's what he saw now, a mix of his imperfect general memory and the slice of memory from the night of the failed prank. Yago wasn't into art like that Miss Blake, but he'd seen paintings by Picasso and that's what the room looked like to him. Everything all jagged and broken into pieces, but somehow making a whole he could recognize.

Yago walked on, stopped at a window in the hall, and looked out. He experienced a brief flicker of nostalgia. Washington, D.C. It had been Yago's town — he'd owned it in some way, been the crown prince. He'd . . .

"Wait a minute," he said aloud.

What he saw from the window was impossible.

Nothing was where it should be. Nothing was in scale. The Washington Monument, that tall needlelike structure, appeared now to be at least twice its normal height. Right next to it, where it shouldn't be, was the Lincoln Memorial, and it was lit as if it were night. Yago blinked. It *was* night, but only around the memorial, not anywhere else. The Washington Monument stood in the full light of day.

*Clop, clop, clop* . . . Yago shot a glance to the left. Horses? Yeah, and some kind of antique carriage, like from that old movie *Gone With the Wind*. And . . . why couldn't he get used to this place? The street on which the horse and carriage rode, the man and woman in the carriage, the horse, the old lampposts, everything was in sepia tone, like the old photographs and tintypes and whatnot Yago had seen when his teacher had dragged the class to the National Gallery and the Smithsonian.

Civil War stuff. Yago didn't like history, but it had pursued him all his life.

He closed his eyes and when he opened them again, where the Lincoln Memorial and Washington Monument had been was something new. Yago squinted and could make out a sign over what looked like a store of some sort. Yes, Maryland Avenue Dry Goods. But there was no dry goods store on Maryland Avenue, and what were dry goods, anyway?

And then he noticed the colors. Not the gray and yellow of the nineteenth-century stuff, but a clearer black and white. Everything seemed more distinct and gentler. The men in large-shouldered, double-breasted suits and hats set at a jaunty angle. The women in hats, too, and short gloves and dresses that came to just below the knee. High heels. Way better than those Civil War clothes.

This was not Yago's time. What he saw out the window was World War II stuff, the early forties, he thought. Yeah, there went a group of navy sailors. And, bizarrely, there was a tank rolling slowly down the middle of the street, turret gun swinging lazily from side to side.

The compression, the distortions . . . The city Yago had remembered and that Mother had re-created was like one of those totally useless maps printed on diner place mats. Maps that highlighted local attractions but gave no information about distance or scale. Maps that had nothing to do with reality.

How would Yago find his way in this D.C.? He fought down a surge of panic, leaned his forehead against the cool pane of window glass. When he stood back, the scene before him had changed again. Clouds of pink . . .

At least the cherry blossoms were in bloom. He'd had no use for winter in D.C. Too gray and dreary. He would make his capital city perpetually warm and bright, always spring or summer.

Yago turned from the window. Enough hanging around. Time to head for the Oval Office. The command center. Time for President Yago Castleman to take control.

# CHAPTER TWELVE

## "WE'RE KILLING HER WITHOUT EVEN TRYING."

Billy had lost his grip on Mother back in the diner, but somehow he was still in touch with her. At least, he thought he was.

He still couldn't trust his thoughts or his feelings or his instincts. Not even his memories, which might actually belong to someone else.

Billy was different. He'd accepted that fact so many years ago, long before the *Mayflower* and the five hundred years of tortuous waking slumber. Long before he'd slowed way, way down, then suddenly speeded up until he was back in sync with normal people.

Sort of.

Was that why the baby hated him so much, Billy

wondered, because he was different? But that made no sense. The baby was different, too.

Anyway, right now Billy was more concerned with Mother than with the baby.

Billy looked at Kubrick and his father. Alberto seemed to be asleep, curled up on the hard floor. Kubrick paced.

Billy would talk to Mo'Steel. He was always full of receptive energy.

"I'm still connected," he said. "I think I might have formed a sort of nonphysical interface with Mother."

Mo'Steel looked interested, so Billy went on.

"It's like I can hear — not with my ears, you know — some faint echo of her thoughts or emotions. She does have thoughts and emotions, even though she's a computer. I can't explain that but I know it's true."

"What else?" Mo'Steel asked.

"Well, every time I hear something, it's like I have to back away." Billy looked at Alberto and Kubrick. Now they were both sitting on the floor, close enough to a pit to be safe from any of the laser projections. Kubrick was silent and brooding. Alberto was awake and mumbling. "Look at what she did to

Alberto," he said quietly. "I don't want to be overwhelmed by her," Billy said with emphasis. "I want to help her. But she's so enormous."

"You did okay back at the diner, 'migo," Mo'Steel said. "Pretty impressive."

Billy felt embarrassed by the compliment. "I was able to resist her probing for a while. But ultimately I couldn't hold her in check. Still, it's like I can't stop hearing a faint, reverberating echo. . . ."

Billy looked at Mo'Steel and smiled ruefully. "Maybe I'm just hearing my own heartbeat. Maybe I'm imagining everything."

Mo'Steel shook his head. "I don't think so, kid. I believe you've got something going on with Mother. So, what's happening with her now?"

"I sensed it before," Billy said, "but now it's clearer." He heard the tension in his own voice. And the exhaustion. "All the new data really are overwhelming her. She was already deranged by boredom and tedium and time. But she'd achieved a sort of stasis."

"She'd made the best of a bad deal."

Billy nodded. "Then she found us and the Children attacked the ship. They've been away so long, they're new to Mother now. So much change, all at once. I . . ."

"What, Billy?"

"We're catalysts for Mother's deterioration," he said sadly. "We're killing her, Mo'Steel. We're killing her without even trying."

# CHAPTER THIRTEEN

## "DON'T EVER STAND ON MY FACE AGAIN."

Yago sat in the high-backed leather chair and allowed himself a grin. Those Secret Service guys in the hall had addressed him as Mr. President. Yeah, that title sat real well with him.

Yago remembered that his mother's Secret Service people had called him an arrogant little boy. Yago burned when he thought of those smug idiots, Agents Horvath and Jackson, who'd let Jobs and 2Face and Mo'Steel get in his face back at Cape Canaveral, just before the *Mayflower* liftoff.

"That was then," Yago reminded himself. "This is now." And this was definitely an improvement. This was the command center of the most important person on the face of the earth.

*No more Earth, buddy.* Okay, but the pathetic remnants of the human race still needed a leader, and Yago had always known he'd make it to the top.

Except he'd never figured on Mother being part of the equation. Yago's mood dropped as low as it had soared high. He owed Mother. He'd like to forget that but he couldn't. It kept coming back to him like greasy burps after a chili dinner. It kept coming back every time he thought of See-Through Man.

*Maybe,* Yago thought, *maybe Mother will cut me some slack, let me settle in a bit, relax, recoup some of my energy. Before she sends me off to do what I promised to do for her. Get rid of the Children.* Yago had no idea at all how he was going to do that.

Whatever he decided to do, Yago knew he was being watched.

Mother could be anywhere. Or everywhere. Making sure he kept his promise.

Maybe that idiot Mo'Steel was right after all. About making a deal with the devil.

There was a knock on the door. Yago was about to yell "Come in," but caught himself. What was the protocol? Okay, this might be only a fantasy, even a nightmare, but it was all he had at the moment. And he was pretty sure the President of the U. S. of A. did not get up to open his own office door. And if anyone had the guts to walk right in without being told . . .

* * *

Mo'Steel wasn't like Jobs, a thinker. But he wasn't stupid. Something was weird, he could feel it, and it wasn't Billy or Kubrick or even poor old Alberto.

"Guys, check this out," he said. He paced while he talked. Had to keep moving. "It's a big coincidence, too big. The Blue Meanies are in exile for a seriously long time. Then right after we're captured they suddenly show up?"

"Stuff just happens sometimes," Kubrick said. He sounded angry. "You don't ask for it to happen, but it does."

Mo'Steel nodded, excited. "Yeah, okay. So the Meanies have been trying to get back into the ship for years and just couldn't do it. Maybe the damage caused by Mother's taking the *Mayflower* into the ship finally made it doable. Accident, sort of."

"Mother unwittingly allowed herself to be vulnerable. Or . . ." Billy mused.

"Or?" Kubrick pressed.

"Or," Mo'Steel said, "there's another player in this game. Someone, or a whole group of someones, who arranged for us and the Meanies to arrive simultaneously. Someone wanting just a good time or something bigger down the line. I don't know."

"The Shipwrights," Billy said.

Mo'Steel shrugged. "Could be. Immediate and

pretty woolly question, 'migos, is how to get back up to the surface with Jobs and all. I mean for real."

A look of exhaustion crept over Billy's face. Kubrick showed nothing. Alberto's mouth was working crazily but nothing was coming out except the occasional grunt and a lot of drool.

Mo'Steel suddenly felt exhausted, too. Was this going to be up to him? He wasn't a leader type. And who did he have to lead, anyway?

Alberto, who was just gone in the head. Kubrick, on the edge with grief and self-revulsion and a big, free-floating anger. Billy was okay in some ways, but unreliable, too. Mo'Steel knew Billy was powerful. But did Billy know how to work his own controls?

The worst part, Mo'Steel realized, was that figuring out how to get back to the surface meant a heck of a lot more than scaling a righteous mountain. It meant going up against a computer a thousand times more advanced than any computer Mo'Steel had known back on Earth. Wasn't his thing, technology.

"Can't we, I don't know, mess up the circuitry somehow? Do something down here to . . ." Kubrick looked around, green eyes narrowed. "The wires or something?"

Mo'Steel laughed. "You're more hopeless than I am."

"Maybe it's really simple," Kubrick said. "Maybe there's one central plug."

"Uh, thanks for the suggestion," Mo'Steel said. "You see a big ole plug, you let me know."

"I'm getting sick of this whole place!" Kubrick shouted. Mo'Steel knew Kubrick wanted to hit something. He wondered if it was going to be him again.

"Why didn't Mother mess you up like she did to my father?" Kubrick demanded, glaring at Billy.

"I think it's because my visions of reality are fluid," Billy said. He was sitting cross-legged on the floor. His tone was musing. "A normal mind, like your father's, is like — an eggshell. It's fairly rigid, so it's easily breakable. My mind has changed during those five hundred years when I was awake and alone, but the real difference was there from the beginning. My mind bends now."

"It's not fair," Kubrick growled. "None of it is fair."

Billy went on as if Kubrick hadn't spoken. "Your father," he said, "is an engineer. His mind was full of rules and measurements and standards. He wasn't prepared for Mother's sense of reality. He couldn't handle her seeing and knowing everything at once, inside and out, from all possible perspectives, past, present, and future." Billy smiled ruefully. "Me, I lived a nightmare for five centuries. If you could call it living. Mother's madness can't shake me. I didn't know that at first, but I do now."

Something came to Mo'Steel. Being down in this crazy basement was turning him into a philosopher or something. "Listen, Billy," he said. "I wonder if your being, uh, you know, different . . ."

"Mo'Steel, by most conventional standards I'm delusional." Billy laughed. "If we were back on Earth I'd be on medication."

Mo'Steel conceded the point. "Okay, maybe that was true. Before. But you don't seem so crazy right now. After your whole thing with Mother, the diner, and all. I mean, if a guy knows he's crazy, is he really crazy?"

"Good question," Billy admitted.

Mo'Steel shrugged. "You might have been the woolliest ride of her life, Billy. We don't know anything about the Shipwrights, right? Maybe craziness is not something they do. That and all the art stuff Mother downloaded, the creatures, the skewed perspectives. Maybe Mother can't handle human lunacy. She was a little messed up, then, *wham,* she swallowed us, talked to you, and went right over the edge."

"And made me better? I don't know."

"Look, maybe we could try it with my dad," Kubrick said, excited. "Expose him to Mother again. Maybe it'll bring him back, right? Shock him into reality. Dragging him around is getting old."

"Whoa." Mo'Steel put up his hands. He had no desire to go experimental on Alberto.

It just didn't seem right.

The door swung open and in strode a man in a Union officer's uniform.

*What,* Yago thought, temper flaring, *was this guy doing barging into the President's office in a Civil War costume?*

"Who are you?" he demanded.

The guy came to a military halt right in the center of the presidential seal woven into the carpet — a seal that boasted an image of Yago's own face — and saluted.

The salute threw Yago. He'd never saluted. Even when his mother's staff told him he had to for some stupid military occasion, he'd refused.

"Who *are* you?" Yago repeated.

"General Philip Sheridan, sir. Reporting that my troops will soon be ready to ride for Manassas."

Yago tried to digest this bit of news.

This scrawny, bowlegged guy was the general of President Yago's armed forces?

Vainly, Yago tried to recall any specifics about General Sheridan. Frankly, he was surprised he'd recognized the name.

Yago made a guess. General Philip Sheridan was not important in a practical way to a twenty-first-century teenager, but for Yago to have stored away his name meant that at some point in time Sheridan had been important to someone.

To the winning side in the War Between the States. The war that had ended slavery, at least on the books. Yago had a personal interest in that subject.

Okay. So he'd listen to what the guy had to say. Just because he was as shrimpy as a ten-year-old didn't necessarily mean he wasn't a good tactician. And though he wasn't ready to admit it, Yago needed all the help he could get.

"What's at Manassas?" he said.

"Sir, the enemy is concentrated there."

"The enemy? What enemy?"

"Why, the Rebels, Mr. President."

"Who told you this? Where do you get your intelligence?" Yago liked the way this sounded.

"My mother told me, sir," the general said. "She told me the Rebels are massed at Manassas."

Yago sneered. A grown man who let his mother tell him . . . and then it hit him. Of course. His mother, Mother. Mother was using this projection of a famous Union general who fought the Rebels, the Confederacy, as a way of bringing Yago to battle against the Children. The Blue Meanies. They were the ones who had rebelled against Mother.

Okay. That much made sense. But as Yago looked at the battle-worn officer before him he realized that he, President Yago, Commander-in-Chief of the Armed Forces, was just not ready to give the order.

Besides, he shouldn't have to go with the troops into battle. The Presidents back on Earth didn't have to associate with the rabble. They had important matters to discuss, big decisions to make.

No, Yago was just not in the mood.

Before Yago could speak, the general said, "Mother says you must accompany the cavalry into battle against the Children. Sir."

Yago blanched. The guy had read his mind! He was the President, he wasn't just someone to be bossed around, by Mother or projection or mutated human.

"Forget it!" he spat. "I'm not going, definitely not now. I just got here. I want to rest, take a bath, watch some TV, grab a bite to eat. Maybe get my hair done. Mother can just . . .

He was . . . he was . . . an animal moan started deep in Yago's chest and by the time it reached his mouth and tongue and lips it erupted as a bellow of panic. He had been buried alive, he was in a casket, laid out between layers of white, perfumed satin. He gagged, felt the tears pouring from the corners of his eyes, tasted the bile. His worst nightmare, the terrible closeness, no air, can't breathe.

Another bellow, he couldn't help it, mind gone now, all alone, only panicpanicpanic . . .

His fingers clutched the edge of the shiny wood desk . . . What? Yago stared at his fingers, pale at the knuckles, then slowly, unbelievingly, raised his eyes, lifted his head. No casket. Not buried alive.

He was in the Oval Office. He was working for Mother. And he was in very deep trouble. Because he knew that if he resisted Mother again, she would punish him again.

Mother had tramped through his subconscious and churned up all of Yago's deepest fears and anxieties and psychological quirks and knew exactly what buttons to push to make him squirm in the most exquisite pain.

"I'm her servant," Yago told himself fiercely. "I'm trapped. I have no power. I have nothing."

Mother had it all.

Yago pushed past General Sheridan.

"Sir? Your orders?"

Yago stopped at the door. Without turning around, he said in his best neutral yet brooking-no-argument voice, "Proceed with your preparations. And don't ever stand on my face again."

# CHAPTER FOURTEEN

## "WHAT HAPPENS TO US IF SHE CRASHES COMPLETELY?"

Billy wasn't surprised Mo'Steel didn't like the idea. He himself was still considering it.

"Even if another interface with Mother doesn't do Alberto much good," Billy said, "it might speed up Mother's deterioration."

*Or,* he added silently, *another encounter might destroy Alberto totally.*

"But is that a good thing?" Mo'Steel argued. "What happens to us if she crashes completely? The roller coaster breaks down and we're tossed into space like a handful of jelly beans."

Billy thought about that. And other things. He felt bad about conspiring to destroy Mother. He understood her as no one else did.

But he'd seen what she'd done to Kubrick. And he knew she was determined to destroy the Blue Meanies. As for using Alberto as a sacrifice, well, it was unlikely he'd ever recover. He wasn't even speaking anymore, just making meaningless sounds.

The fact was that Mother was dangerous.

The answer seemed clear to Billy. At the same time, the answer disturbed him deep down. You could know what you had to do and still choose not to do it, right?

*But I'm the crazy one,* he thought. *So what do I know?*

Yago stood in the hallway outside the Oval Office. General Sheridan had gone outside to his troops. What did "outside" really mean here? Eventually, he'd have to venture into the distortions and find out.

Yago rubbed his temples. The others were all pretty much idiots and losers, but right now, for the first time since coming out of hibernation, Yago felt lonely for the presence of another human being. Not a projection like Sheridan, but another flesh and blood . . .

Yago's hands dropped. Voices? Yes. Coming from . . .

Yago whirled. Where the door to the Oval Office had been there was a different door. And the voices, angry, confused, were coming from . . .

He strode to the door and yanked it open. It was the Cabinet room, he recognized it. And inside, clustered like scared sheep, were some of the other survivors of the *Mayflower*.

D-Caf, the little worm. But useful in some ways, an aspiring toady. Junior sycophant. Then, the bizarro world's madonna and child, Sergeant Tamara Hoyle and the baby. Olga Gonzalez, Monkey Boy's mother. Burroway, the astrophysicist with an ego the size of the Grand Canyon and the pampered whine of a serious weenie. T.R. A shrink.

The other kids, Roger Dodger and Tate and that brute, Anamull. The Dodger kid seemed harmless enough. The girl, Tate, had gone against the idea of sacrificing one of them to the baby, back at the tower. She'd called them all cowards. *Better watch her,* Yago thought. Anamull, yeah, he could come in handy. Guy seemed okay with taking orders.

*Mother was keeping her part of the bargain*, Yago thought angrily. He didn't even need to open his mouth to get what he wanted. If what he wanted met with Mother's approval. A pizza with pepperoni? No doubt he could ask for that and it would be on the table before him, steaming hot and fresh from the oven. A ticket out of this stifling bargain with the devil? He'd be back in the coffin.

For a moment Yago stood staring at the group, wondering if he would be better off asking Mother to send them back to wherever they'd come from. But no. He was the President and a pitiful staff was better than no staff.

Besides, Tamara and the baby were some kind of outrageously powerful fighting machine. Yago had to keep that unit at least, but he didn't necessarily want to be alone with the freakish duo. There was relative safety in numbers.

"What happened?" Burroway demanded, breaking the sudden silence that Yago's appearance had caused. Yago had to restrain himself from laughing out loud. With his balding head and hawklike nose, Burroway looked like a big pathetic bird.

Yago said coolly, "Where should I begin?"

"One minute we're on the *Constitution,*" Burroway raged on, "the next minute we're being shot at by soldiers . . ."

"It was a varied landscape." T.R.'s normally lilting voice was comically high with anxiety. "I believe it was an American city. . . ."

"Austin," Olga said. "Texas. I think."

Yago noted her relative calm. She was a rational sort. Unlike her son.

"Then everything just disappeared," Tate said. "It was like . . . a void. Except for one far-off point of light."

Roger Dodger nodded. "Yeah, it was coming from a restaurant, I think. Got anything to eat in this place?"

Yago ignored the kid's question. "It was a diner, actually," he said. "Booths, a counter, bad coffee, the usual. Waiter didn't deserve a tip but I'm a generous sort of guy."

Burroway gave him a look of outrage. T.R. seemed confused. The guys had no sense of humor.

"You haven't seen my son?" Olga asked now.

"He's fine," Yago said. "At least he was last time I saw him. In the diner."

Olga nodded. "Romeo can take care of himself."

Olga's obvious pride in her son infuriated Yago.

"This is what's going on," he said abruptly. He told them what he knew, leaving out, of course, the more embarrassing parts, like his own doubt about the wisdom of the decision he'd made to assist Mother.

"Bottom line," he finished, "this is the White House and I am the President. General Philip Sheridan is preparing to ride against the Blue Meanies at

Manassas. We're going with him," he said, looking pointedly at Tamara. "Any questions?"

There were none. There was only stunned silence.

And then, the baby let out its horrible, high-pitched giggle.

# CHAPTER FIFTEEN

## "WHO TOLD YOU YOU MATTERED, YAGO?"

They were milling around an area that looked something like Yago's grammar school courtyard. He and the other Remnants had little to do. General Sheridan and his men were saddling up the horses, cleaning and loading guns, hoisting cannons onto wagons.

The courtyard was paved with cobblestones. The sharp clomping of the horses' shoes on the stones was driving Yago nuts. Every whinny cut through his head like a scream.

Yago wanted nothing more than to reverse the clock and this time keep his mouth shut when Mother made her offer. Anything but be where he was, facing what he was facing.

War.

The panic, he had to fight it down. This was worse than when he'd been put into the tiny berth on the *Mayflower.*

Worse than hallucinating he'd been buried alive.

Worse than the claustrophobia that had haunted him since he was a little kid, since that rainy night he'd accidentally fallen into the big hole a workman had dug in the backyard, since the muddy walls of the hole had collapsed in on him, since he'd been trapped in the wet and the dark, invisible, too panicked to cry out, convinced he was going to die.

They hadn't found him until morning.

It was choking him, the panic, he was going to vomit it all up. For a second Yago considered doing just that, sneaking off and letting the panic come pouring out of him.

But he couldn't allow that. Okay, maybe his decision to help Mother was foolish. But he'd made the decision, so he'd have to live with it.

Yago strode over to Tamara and the baby, took Tamara's elbow, and released it like he'd been burned. Too gross, with that freak kid on her hip.

He nodded instead, indicating she should follow him a few feet away from the others. She did.

"Look," Yago said, trying not to focus on the baby but on the blank face of its mother. "I'm running things now, Sergeant. I'm in charge. Everyone takes orders from me. I'm in tight with Mother, okay, she and I have a deal. Stick with me, you can have whatever you want." He nodded reluctantly to the baby. "Whatever you both want."

The freakish thing in the soldier's arms grinned that horrifying grin and Yago took a shuddering step back. *Look at the mother, Yago,* he commanded silently. *Not at the teeth . . .*

He did. Her face was still blank.

"The baby wants your arm," she said, like she was saying, "It's going to rain today."

Yago's mouth dropped open and he shot a look at the baby. It licked its lips.

Yago clapped a hand to his mouth and felt his stomach heave.

And then Tamara laughed, but it was a mirthless, empty laugh. "Relax. It's only the baby's little joke," she said. "Look, you are the boss of no one, least of all the baby. Do you understand, Yago? You are Mother's tool, not her colleague. The baby knows this. The baby will deal with Mother when the time comes. Directly. The baby has no need for you. Who told you you mattered, Yago?"

"I can get you what you want," he said again, and his voice cracked. "Whatever it is you want."

Tamara adjusted the baby on her slim hip. She sighed. "The baby does not need you."

Yago stood, mortified, furious, impotent, and watched them walk away.

Jobs had been just about to bite into a shiny red apple when suddenly he found himself no longer an unwelcome guest at a post-concert party but staring up at the Jefferson Memorial. Washington, D.C. Or Yago's version of it.

"Here we go again," 2Face had said. She'd sounded annoyed.

Jobs was, too.

He did not want to be dragged further into Yago's personal psychodrama. But he did want to know what was going on. Information was essential.

So Jobs, 2Face, Miss Blake, and Edward had walked through the strange town that was comprised of people and buildings from various decades of the nineteenth and twentieth centuries. They'd walked on concrete and through mud and over brick and cobblestones until they'd found Yago.

Yago was at the White House. Miss Blake had raised an eyebrow and said, "Of course."

Now they were watching Yago's play unfold from a hiding place. It wasn't completely secure but so far everyone in the courtyard had been too busy to look behind the early twenty-first-century SUV parked near the entrance to the street.

Jobs saw that someone other than Yago was in charge of the cavalry. Yago seemed superfluous next to the short, intense man in uniform. And the bars on the shoulders of his coat meant the man was an officer. Beyond that, Jobs didn't know what was going on.

Jobs watched as the officer shouted orders to three soldiers securing cannons on a wooden wagon.

"I wonder," he said, "if that guy is really someone from history. Maybe he's from a novel Yago once read."

2Face laughed. "Yago, read?"

"Yago must have paid more attention in history class than we assume he did," Miss Blake said. "I guess I did, too. That's General Philip Henry Sheridan. One of the most ruthless Union commanders of the Civil War."

"No wonder Yago remembered him," 2Face said. "Probably one of his heroes."

"Maybe," Miss Blake said. "But are these troops equipped to go up against the Blue Meanies? They're six centuries apart in applied technology."

Jobs watched Yago and the others mount their horses. Most needed help.

Burroway's foot kept slipping out of the stirrup.

T.R. barely had the strength to pull himself up into the saddle.

Anamull threw himself so heavily on his horse, he came close to tumbling off the far side.

Olga Gonzalez did okay. So did Tate. Roger Dodger let himself be lifted.

D-Caf made it, but awkwardly. Yago did okay, too, but he sat uncomfortably in the saddle.

Tamara, still holding the baby, easily mounted her horse, using only one hand to hoist the combined weight.

"Except for Tamara and the baby, they'll probably be slaughtered," Jobs said. "How are pistols and swords going to take down flying aliens in armor? And cannons can't hit moving targets."

"Well, the Union soldiers have experience," 2Face said. "Unless they've been called up out of Yago's head with no other input from Mother."

"She might have put Yago's memories together with information from a data disc," Miss Blake suggested.

Jobs watched as General Sheridan gave the signal and Yago and the other Remnants rode off at the head of the regiment of Union cavalry. Yago's mouth was set in a grim line. The others looked deeply afraid.

"So, where exactly are they going?" 2Face said.

Miss Blake shook her head. "Should we follow them?"

"I could go."

Jobs looked down at his little brother.

"What?"

Edward shrugged. "I could find out stuff. They won't see me 'cause I won't look like me."

Jobs looked at Miss Blake and 2Face. "What do you think?" he said.

2Face crouched in front of Edward and put her hands on his shoulders. "Okay, kid. But you have to be really careful."

"If they go into battle," Miss Blake said, "stay out of it."

Edward was Jobs's responsibility. He wasn't sure he should let Edward go, but if Miss Blake thought it was okay, it was probably okay. "Thanks, Edward."

Edward smiled and scurried off. Jobs watched his little brother sneak up close to a slow-moving group of packhorses at the rear of the regiment's column and suddenly seemed to disappear. He blended right into the pack of horses.

"Okay," he said. "What now?"

2Face grinned. "Taxi!"

# CHAPTER SIXTEEN

## "IT'S YAGO'S DAD!"

2Face shut the front passenger side door behind her. Jobs and Violet were in the backseat, Jobs behind the driver.

The cab was more of a sports car, 2Face noted. The backseat was practically in the front seat.

"Look, we . . ."

2Face stopped. Stared at the driver's profile. He turned to look at her, his expression quizzical. 2Face glanced at the identification card on the dashboard. Yeah, same guy. But . . .

"Uh, Mr. Castleman?"

"That's my name, don't wear it out." The driver chuckled.

"It's Yago's dad!" 2Face hissed over her shoulder.

"Don't have no kids," the driver said nonchalantly. "Never married. Never got around to it. What kind of a name is Yago, anyway? What about a nice, normal name, like, say, Robert?"

2Face said, "Right. Uh, we need to follow the cavalry."

"Stop!"

Mr. Castleman slammed on the brakes. The cab screeched to a stop.

"We have to pick up Edward," Jobs said, pointing to the horse.

"Now you just wait a minute, son." Mr. Castleman looked over his shoulder. "Do you know what a horse can do to fine leather upholstery? Plus, I don't know. He looks awfully big."

2Face rolled her eyes. "Just please open your window, sir."

Mr. Castleman did.

"Edward?!" Jobs called.

"I don't want any damage to the paint, either," Mr. Castleman mumbled. Then, "What the . . . where did it go?"

Miss Blake threw open the mini third door behind the front passenger side door. "Edward, get in!"

Edward scampered around the front of the cab and climbed in over Miss Blake. He squeezed himself in between her and Jobs.

"Don't leave yet, Mr. Castleman," Jobs said. The man grunted. Jobs turned to Edward. "Well, did you hear anything? Where are they going?"

Edward frowned. "Um, it was a weird word. They were all saying it."

"Saying what?" 2Face said. "C'mon, Edward, think."

Edward smiled, like he'd just remembered. "They were saying as how they're going to crush the Rebels. At Manastis."

"Manassas? Is that what they said?" Jobs prodded.

Edward replied, "Maybe. Someplace where there are Rebels."

"Manassas," Miss Blake said. "It was the site of several Civil War battles."

"Who usually won?" Jobs asked.

"The Rebels."

"In this case," Jobs said, "the Blue Meanies."

2Face was grim. "We told Yago not to make a deal with Mother —"

"But he did," Jobs interrupted, "so now what do we do? Do we help Yago? Or do we stay out of it?"

"We didn't promise Mother we'd kill the Blue Meanies," Miss Blake said. "Yago did."

"What difference does it make now whether we

join in?" 2Face raged. "Mother won't stop until she's eliminated the Meanies. If Yago can't accomplish the extinction, she'll find some other way. And we'll be punished along with Yago."

"And if Yago does keep his promise . . ."

"We're done," 2Face said. "If he comes out a hero, he's in charge of us all. I've said from the start that Yago is our number one enemy."

Jobs had been through this with 2Face before. Most times he wasn't sure he trusted 2Face any more than he did Yago. "Yago is as much a pawn as we are," he said.

"But . . ."

Miss Blake put her hand on 2Face's shoulder and Jobs was surprised to see that such a seemingly gentle act of restraint had its desired effect.

He went on. "But I agree our being captives of a malfunctioning computer can't go on. Mother has to be disconnected."

Jobs turned to Miss Blake. "What do you think?"

"The enemy of my enemy is my friend," she said carefully. "At least for the duration of the fight. None of us know enough about the Blue Meanies to trust them beyond what we think is their immediate goal — get to Mother. But maybe that's all we need to know, for now."

Jobs thought he'd been wrong before, like when he'd banked on that "enemy of my enemy" thing, back when he'd ordered an attack on the Squids to show solidarity with the Blue Meanies. Still . . .

"Let's go to Manassas," he said finally. "We'll try to forge an alliance with the Blue Meanies."

Mr. Castleman frowned. "Manassas? That's going to be a hefty fare. You kids have the money?"

Miss Blake laughed. "Sure."

"Pedal to the metal, Mr. Castleman, sir," 2Face said. "We need to get to Manassas before the cavalry."

# CHAPTER SEVENTEEN

## "FOUR SACRED STREAMS WAS OUR FRIEND."

"Here you are," Mr. Castleman said. "Manassas."

Jobs's eyes widened. "Are you sure?"

Mr. Castleman half turned in his seat. "I've been working this route for ten years, kid. If I say this is Manassas, it's Manassas."

"Fine, thanks," 2Face said. She pushed open the front passenger side door and got out. The others followed.

"It's a sports stadium," Miss Blake said, squinting up at the massive structure. Behind them the cab pulled away.

Jobs nodded. A stadium, but with the usual distortions they'd come to expect. The environment was a combination of Yago's memory and Mother's imperfect research. For example, there was a massive barn door where no barn door should be. And the outer walls were painted in swirls of pink and purple and lime green.

"Football stadium," 2Face confirmed. "For the Washington Warriors, formerly the Redskins. I had an uncle who was into football."

"Can we get a hot dog?" Edward asked.

"I think it's up to them," Jobs said. "Look."

Atop the stadium's walls Blue Meanies were posted. Jobs counted six sentinels and assumed there were more on the far side of the stadium.

"How do we get in?" Miss Blake said.

"First," Jobs said, "we let them know we've come in peace." But would the Blue Meanies understand him? They didn't have Billy to facilitate communication.

Jobs cleared his throat and looked up at the Blue Meanie positioned directly in his line of sight.

"We have a message from one of your people," he shouted. "From Four Sacred Streams. He asked us to, uh, sing to his people of his death. He died destroying node thirty-one. We are friends," Jobs added, a bit embarrassed to be shouting all this. "Four Sacred Streams was our friend."

Jobs, 2Face, Miss Blake, and Edward stood motionless in the muggy air and waited. None of the Blue Meanies on the stadium walls stirred.

"Well," 2Face said under her breath. "What now?"

And then the huge barn doors slowly began to open.

"Show time," Miss Blake said softly.

Noyze watched guards lead the two boys and two girls onto the playing field. From up in the cheap seats nothing about them seemed familiar. But of course the four had been on the *Mayflower*.

Noyze scrambled ten rows closer to the field and ducked. She felt her heart pumping in her chest.

The four kids stopped in front of Twelve Hallowed Stones. Noyze had no doubt he'd understood what the older boy had called out from below. She also knew he wasn't going to let on that he'd understood their message.

Noyze watched the older boy and the blond girl gesturing, mouths moving, trying to communicate. For a second Noyze lost sight of the little boy. Then she saw him again, standing close to one of the Children.

The dark-haired girl with the scarred face peered around suspiciously.

Noyze turned away and snuck off. She would find Dr. Cohen. Together they would find a way to speak to the new captives.

Maybe together they could all find a way to stay alive.

* * *

Twelve Hallowed Stones did not judge the humans to be an immediate threat. So he had dismissed three to wander the camp and indicated he would listen to the light-haired female alone. Too many human voices at once unnerved him.

The light-haired female squatted in the dirt and with the stick she had requested — which Twelve Hallowed Stones had provided — began to draw.

The female spoke as she drew, and periodically looked up at Twelve Hallowed Stones intently, willing him to understand. He did understand, of course, but remained impassive.

First the female drew a simple figure that represented some of the humans. Twelve Hallowed Stones knew this because the female gestured to herself and to the others she'd come with. Besides, he recognized the words she spoke.

"Us," she'd said, counting off four fingers. "Me and my companions." Clearly she did not know of the existence of the other humans Twelve Hallowed Stones had been guarding.

Then the female drew a crude four-legged figure and pointed to him. Twelve Hallowed Stones repressed a flicker of annoyance.

The young female went on to draw figures that

represented humans other than those present in the Children's camp. Those on the battleship, Twelve Hallowed Stones guessed.

"And Mother," she said, looking up at him. Twelve Hallowed Stones watched as the female drew a distinctly human, feminine form, large and round. It was nothing like Mother, but Twelve Hallowed Stones understood.

What was the human trying to tell him? Twelve Hallowed Stones wished she would just speak and not waste time playing in the dirt.

Carefully the female drew a large circle that encompassed the other humans and Mother.

"They have joined forces," she said. "Mother — well, she is making these humans attack you. They're being forced to attempt to destroy you."

Twelve Hallowed Stones watched as the female drew a thin jagged line, tipped with an arrow, from the large circle to the figure representing the Children. She continued the jagged line all around the figure, until it was enclosed.

"Do you understand?" she said. "The humans are not your enemies."

Twelve Hallowed Stones gave no sign of understanding. But he did understand and in spite of himself was impressed with the young female's ability to communicate the notion of alliances. What she'd said regarding the humans being forced to march against the Children interested him. He was not sure if he believed it. He was not sure it made a difference.

Twelve Hallowed Stones looked down at the female, still kneeling in the dirt. The Children would save Mother. They would save themselves.

The humans would have to be sacrificed.

Violet was frustrated. She thought this alien understood what she was trying to communicate. But he gave no indication of comprehension, no indication of anything at all.

If only Billy were there.

Violet was frustrated but scared, too.

"I am going back to my friends," she said, and pointed first to herself, then over her shoulder.

She took a step back. The Blue Meanie just stood there. So Violet turned her back to him and walked away.

# CHAPTER EIGHTEEN

"WE'RE THE ENEMY IN THE ENEMY CAMP."

Nobody had locked them up. Jobs thought it was odd but wasn't complaining. The Blue Meanies were letting them walk around free.

Still, Jobs had some hope for a deal with the Blue Meanies. They didn't seem totally unreasonable.

While Miss Blake remained to communicate with one of the aliens, Edward had gone with 2Face to look for food. Jobs opted to stay on the edge of the playing field, close to Miss Blake.

That's when he saw them. They were watching him from the interior end of a long corridor. Jobs took a few steps closer to the opening of the corridor.

A girl, small and dark skinned, her hair pulled back tightly in a short ponytail, and a woman, slim, medium height, with light brown hair tucked behind her ears. Jobs wondered if they were real or

Mother's projections or images called up from the stew in Yago's head.

Only one way to find out. Jobs walked toward the girl and the woman. They watched him come.

When he was within fifteen feet of them, the girl smiled. "I remember you," she said. "I saw you and your parents and a little boy. At the barracks. I'd forgotten."

"You were on the *Mayflower,*" Jobs said, less a question than a statement.

"Dr. Angelique Cohen," the woman said, extending her hand.

Jobs took it, introduced himself. He wondered how much these two knew of what had happened to their families. He would spare them the gory details of the Cheesers, the Wormers, the Facelifts.

"I'm Noyze," the girl said. "Where did you come from? Dr. Cohen and I woke up prisoners of the Children."

Jobs smiled. "We've been calling them the Blue Meanies. Because of the color of the suits."

Dr. Cohen raised an eyebrow.

Jobs shrugged. "We've been wandering. Mostly in two groups."

"Who's with you?" Dr. Cohen asked eagerly. "Is there a Dr. Alan Carrington? He's my husband."

Noyze looked steadily at Jobs but didn't ask about anyone.

Jobs felt uncomfortable.

"No," he said. Then added quickly, "But we know there were eight people missing from the ship. We assumed they'd been taken away by someone. You and Noyze are two. That means there are six others, but we don't know who they are."

Dr. Cohen's lips tightened and she nodded.

"Your parents?" Noyze said, her voice gentle.

The simple question opened the floodgates of sadness. So much loss. How could he ever forget? "They didn't make it," he said. "But Edward, my little brother, did."

"That's good."

"Why Noyze?" he said with his almost smile.

"Mostly deaf until I was twelve," Noyze said simply. "After that . . ."

Jobs nodded.

He spotted 2Face and Edward farther along the concourse and waved to them. When they joined the group, Jobs made quick introductions. He noted 2Face glance at Noyze out of the corner of her eye, almost warily.

"Be careful what you say around the Blue Meanies," Noyze warned. "Your friend is talking to Twelve

Hallowed Stones. He understands some human speech. They've designated us as enemies."

"Why?" Jobs asked, though he could guess the answer.

Noyze frowned. "They're jealous of us. They call themselves Mother's True Children. But they see Mother favoring us somehow. What are they supposed to feel?"

"We don't want to be Mother's Children," Jobs explained unnecessarily. "Mother's damaged. The Blue Meanies want to fix her so they're welcomed again. We want to fix her so we're not her pawns anymore. Our goal doesn't conflict with the Meanies' goal."

"We're still the outsiders," 2Face said. "If the Meanies get to Mother first, do you think they're going to opt for peaceable coexistence? No way. It'll still be us against them."

"2Face is right," Dr. Cohen said.

"It shouldn't be that way," Jobs said. "They assume we're invaders when actually we're captives."

"Noyze," 2Face challenged, "do the Meanies have any weaknesses we can exploit? Anything they want badly enough that we can give them?"

Noyze looked to Dr. Cohen.

"Nothing we noticed," Dr. Cohen said. "Except

for the fact that out of their suits the Children are fairly defenseless."

Jobs watched as Miss Blake approached through the same corridor he'd taken. He introduced her.

"I couldn't get anywhere with him," she said worriedly. "Assuming he understood what I was trying to say. I don't see how we can get them to commit to an alliance."

"We're the enemy in the enemy camp," 2Face said grimly. "Totally vulnerable."

Suddenly, there was a loud whirring or chirping, like the unexpected cacophony of cicadas on a summer night. Jobs, Miss Blake, 2Face, and Edward raced back onto the playing field, following Noyze and Dr. Cohen. Five of the Blue Meanies hovered in the air, their tentacles working madly.

"They're sounding an alarm," Noyze said. "We're being attacked."

# CHAPTER NINETEEN

## "THIS IS GOING TO BE AWESOME."

The entire thing was insane. He was a kid from the twenty-first century, wearing a modified Union officer's uniform from the nineteenth century, about to throw down with a bunch of aliens in the twenty-sixth century, who were, Yago just knew, really, really ticked off.

This was not in the game plan, any of it. And the worst thing was there was no way of escaping Mother's clutches. Once you were in, there was no way out. Oh, except one. Death.

The cavalry had stopped about a mile away from some huge structure that Yago recognized as the Washington Warriors' stadium. Sort of. The real Warriors' stadium wasn't decorated like some psychedelic trip. What in his subconscious had created *that*?

Back in his old life Yago had had season tickets to every home game, stellar seats in the skybox. Security for Yago and his family and friends at those big public events had been a royal pain but Yago dealt with it.

Yago watched General Sheridan's men unlimbering the cannons. They were going to fight the super-advanced alien enemy with cannons and bayonets and slingshots, for all he knew. One of the soldiers even carried a bugle. Another one carried a huge flag with an ugly mix of stars, stripes, and Yago's smiling face.

At least he wasn't the only one looking distinctly uncomfortable. Yago had always been able to get satisfaction out of others' misery. He had that going for him.

Burroway. The guy was clearly petrified. Yago had seen him throwing up behind one of the munitions wagons. Now he stood, mouth clamped shut, T.R. jabbering away next to him. No doubt T.R. was trying to convince Burroway they should make a break for it.

What they didn't know was that with Mother, there was no making a break.

Or was there? Would Mother care if they ran

off, as long as Yago remained on the battlefield, keeping his promise?

"You, Burroway, T.R.," Yago called, striding toward the two men. "Stop standing around and report to General Sheridan."

Burroway's eyes got that indignant look. The one that tried unsuccessfully to mask fear.

"That's an order," Yago growled. "Failure to carry out an order from your commanding officer will result in court-martial."

Where had he gotten that? Some movie. Anyway, the threat worked. Burroway and T.R. scurried off, T.R.'s too-long uniform pants flapping around his ankles.

"Yago, man!"

It was Anamull, slow-jogging toward him. Anamull was sweating even more than Yago in his ill-fitting, not quite standard-issue wool uniform. Why Mother had insisted they wear them, through a message from Sheridan, Yago couldn't guess. Maybe Mother had a sense of humor after all.

"This is going to be awesome," Anamull shouted.

Yago cringed. "I'm standing right here, idiot," he said. "Go assist the . . . those soldiers." He pointed.

Anamull didn't seem to mind the reprimand. He

bounded off toward a small group of soldiers who were cleaning their rifles.

"Yago!"

Yago almost groaned aloud. Why didn't they all just leave him alone? Now it was Tate, toting a rifle over her left shoulder, pinning him with her eyes.

"What is it, soldier?" Yago barked.

"I don't know why exactly we're doing this," Tate said, staring hard at Yago. "Why should we help Mother when she's the cause of all this craziness? But if someone attacks you, you fight back. That I understand. So if the Blue Meanies fire first, I'll fire back in self-defense. Not because I'm obeying your command. I want to be clear on that. After what you tried back at the tower, I don't trust you, Yago."

"Okay, fine," he mumbled, turning away before he said something stupid.

"Yago!"

Olga Gonzalez. Yago sighed. She was another problem.

Yago turned and waited until she slipped and slid her way up the dune.

"I'm not going to fight, Yago," she said. "I'm a conscientious objector. You can't make me participate in an act of aggression or violence."

"Fine," he snapped. "But as long as I'm in charge, you'll make yourself useful. Somehow. Don't go far. Stay with the medics."

Olga didn't respond to his order. She just turned and slid back down the dune. Yago did not have a lot of faith in her loyalty.

At this moment, Yago did not have a lot of faith in anybody. Least of all, himself.

# CHAPTER TWENTY

THINGS WERE ONLY GETTING WORSE.

"Don't look now, but we're surrounded."

2Face spoke very quietly. It seemed the right thing to do under the circumstances. Standing unprotected out in the open like they were, a menacing circle of Blue Meanies forming.

"Suddenly, I don't feel so good," Dr. Cohen said, with a nervous laugh. "Maybe it's the sun."

2Face saw another Blue Meanie pop up in the bleachers. And another.

"Or maybe it's the fact that we're about to be skewered," 2Face said. "So, do we stand here like idiots or do we haul butt out of here?"

"Follow me," Noyze said. "I know this place best of all. If we can't escape maybe we can hide."

"Back in through the corridor?" Jobs said.

Noyze nodded. "On three. One. Two. Three!"

The six turned and ran straight for the corridor.

Jobs tripped over a hanging shred of Violet's skirt. Dr. Cohen stumbled over her own feet.

"Go, go, go!" 2Face shouted. She didn't want to but she hung back and herded the others ahead of her, across the field, into the relative darkness of the corridor. Too close behind her, 2Face heard the whirring and clatter of the Meanies as they followed.

"Which way?" Jobs cried when the corridor opened onto the concourse.

Noyze pointed left and everyone took off again.

2Face pumped her legs, lifting them high, feet slapping down on tile over concrete. She figured she was the only one of the group who might be able to outrun one of the Blue Meanies — maybe. Already she'd passed Noyze. Well, they were all on their own. Except maybe for the kid, Edward. She'd do what she could to help him.

2Face ran past concession stands closed tight, metal gates drawn down from the ceiling to the floor and locked. Hot boiled peanuts, supersized sodas, cotton candy, beer. Behind her, the *slap slap slap* of feet.

There had to be a place to hide! To wait out this stupid battle until the environment shifted again and they found themselves someplace else.

Anyplace but here.

* * *

"This is for you, Mr. President."

Yago whirled.

General Sheridan stood with him on the dune. He held out a stubby-looking sword in its scabbard.

"What is it?" Yago asked stupidly.

"Mr. President, this is a Roman-style artillery short sword. This weapon allows a man to get up close to his enemy and gut him up under the ribs. Highly effective for hand-to-hand combat."

"Can I . . ." Yago swallowed hard. He tried again. "I want a regular sword," he said, trying to stare forcefully at the little general.

General Sheridan's face remained impassive but Yago knew the man was mocking him inside.

"You are to have both, Mr. President." Sheridan produced a weapon from behind his back like cartoon figures produced signs — automatically and impossibly. "We call this magnificent weapon Old Wristbreaker. You won't go wrong with this, sir."

Yago nodded. Things were only getting worse. He put out his hand for the short sword and buckled it on. Then he took the saber. The weight made his wrist collapse weakly. Old Wristbreaker was right. He'd never be able to use this thing.

"One more essential piece, Mr. President," General Sheridan said. "Your Remington revolver. A fine pistol."

Yago took that, too, and slipped it under his belt.

"Now you're ready to ride against the enemy," General Sheridan pronounced.

*No,* Yago protested silently. *No, I'm not.*

*Yes, you are. You are ready. I have helped you. I have made sure.*

*And you will be victorious, human with the strange eyes.*

*You promised me you would be victorious.*

"We are ready to begin firing."

"What? I mean, very good, General. You may give the order."

General Sheridan squinted up at Yago. "Sir, with all due respect, it's your job to give the order to bombard the Rebel stronghold."

"Of course. Right." Yago glanced around for Tamara and the baby but he couldn't spot them amid the shifting crowd of soldiers and horses and cannons.

He was on his own.

Yago and General Sheridan left the dune and approached the soldiers lined up behind the row of ten cannons.

Yago cleared his throat. General Sheridan was watching him. The team of soldiers at each cannon was waiting.

"Fire!" he yelled.

*Ba-BOOM! Ba-BOOM!*

Cannon after cannon fired, was reloaded, fired again. And the stadium walls began to be pockmarked with holes. Yago watched, fascinated. The walls were crumbling. They had looked so strong but they were falling down into piles of concrete rubble and rebar. Clouds of smoke and dust billowed up from the wreckage.

"This just might work," Yago whispered. Adrenaline surged through his body. He was responsible for this destruction. He was in charge.

"Blast open the main entrance!" he shouted.

# CHAPTER TWENTY-ONE

## IT FELT LIKE BEING THE KING.

*Ba-BOOM! Ba-BOOM!*

Violet's eyes closed and her shoulders hunched and her hands clenched with every blast.

The sound of cannon fire was a weapon in and of itself. She hadn't liked it back on the *Constitution* and she didn't like it now.

Edward whimpered and Violet put her arm around him. They were huddled behind the counter of a twisty-pretzel stand. Violet read the menu up on the wall. Caramel pretzels. Extra-salt pretzels. Bubble-gum pretzels. Ugh.

*I would do anything for a piece of grilled swordfish,* Violet thought. *And a new pair of shoes. Patent leather would be nice.*

"This is ridiculous," 2Face whispered. "You couldn't find anyplace safer?"

Noyze's eyes were wide with fear. "Everything's locked. I don't know why. I've gotten in the bathrooms and the janitor closets and the storerooms before."

"They were prepared," Dr. Cohen said.

"Better prepared than we gave them credit for," Violet added.

Jobs rose carefully to peer over the edge of the counter. He dropped quickly. "Blue Meanie, coming this way."

"Obviously, hiding is not the answer," 2Face said, her voice barely audible.

"So, we keep running?" Violet shot a glance upward, half expecting to see a Blue Meanie leaning on the counter, watching them.

2Face nodded. "Until Yago and his troops blast their way in. Then we can join up with them."

Noyze suddenly tensed. She rolled her eyes in the direction of the concourse, beyond the counter.

The Blue Meanie. Violet knew there was no reason for him to look behind this particular counter. She also knew there was no reason for him not to.

Miraculously, the Meanie passed by. After a moment Jobs snuck another look and came back with a thumbs-up. But his expression was serious.

"Okay," Violet mouthed. "We fight."

Suddenly, a different sound. She cocked her head and put a finger to her lips.

There it was. Unmistakable. The sound of a bugle. The sound of a charge.

"Mr. President!" Yago turned to see General Sheridan draw his sword. "It's time to mount up! You will lead the charge."

Yago grinned. He couldn't believe he'd been so afraid. As far as he could tell, they were totally winning. He hadn't seen one Blue Meanie fire back.

Yago got on his horse. It was a chestnut mare with a black mane and tail. Yago liked how it felt sitting atop the beautiful animal. It felt like being the king.

He surveyed his troops. Tamara and the baby were seated on a massive gray horse that looked more built for endurance than speed. The others, on their mounts, hung back behind the Union soldiers.

For a second Yago considered pulling out Old Wristbreaker and leading the regiment like a real soldier. But if the sword was out he might be expected to use it. Instead, Yago took the Remington from his belt. His horse suddenly began to dance nervously. Yago yanked on the reins to steady her.

And before he could issue the command, the horse bolted. Yago's neck snapped and his head was whipped back. "Ch-ch-charge," he called, and was aware of the sudden thunder of hooves behind him.

Yago stuffed the pistol back into his belt and grabbed the reins with two hands. "Slow down!" he yelled. "Whoa!" But the horse kept racing toward the bombed entrance of the stadium.

Yago was leading the charge, just like Mother wanted.

He held on.

When he was within several yards of the entrance Yago saw them. Blue Meanies swooping low, gathering, waiting.

Again he yanked back on the reins but his horse paid no attention.

And then they were in!

And a thick swarm of — what? — was blanketing him. Yago screamed as his skin was pierced by thousands of tiny, razor-sharp pieces of metal.

His horse reared wildly. Yago grabbed tighter with his knees and pressed his upper body against the horse's neck. Fléchettes tore through the worn wool of his uniform and lacerated his back. Then the horse's front hooves clattered back to earth and Yago couldn't believe he hadn't been thrown.

"Aaggghhh!"

A soldier down. Another one, just behind Yago.

And then — a Blue Meanie careening wildly toward the ground. Yago hadn't seen what had hit him but he was fiercely glad to see the alien crash.

"C'mon!" he urged, and this time, the horse understood. Yago crouched low and they galloped farther into the stadium, onto the playing field, across white chalk lines and toward the goalposts. Away from the front gates.

Right into a wall of Blue Meanies, dropping out of the air, fléchette guns aimed straight at Yago.

He heard General Sheridan shouting, "Fire! Fire!" and thought, *Why? What was the use?*

They'd followed the sounds of the battle out onto the playing field. Blue Meanies hovered and dove and fired into the soldiers on the ground.

It took Jobs about two seconds to see that the Meanies were winning.

"Everybody grab a weapon," 2Face ordered. They left Edward hidden behind the front row of spectator seats.

Jobs ran toward a uniformed body sprawled on its stomach.

Jobs froze.

"What's wrong?"

It was Miss Blake. Jobs turned to her and opened his mouth to say something but no words came out.

Miss Blake looked quickly from Jobs to the dead soldier and back again. "This is not the time for sentiment," she said harshly. "Besides, he's not even real. We are. Come on, Jobs. We need you."

Miss Blake didn't wait around.

Jobs got to his feet. He had the weapon.

And he heard the scream. The sound was awful, ripping through him with the viciousness of deliberate torture.

Jobs whirled. It was Yago! His horse was down, still screaming, legs twitching. Yago was crying, sobbing, desperately trying to pull his left leg out from under the thousand or so pounds of animal.

Jobs raced toward Yago, vaguely aware of what he had to do. When he reached Yago he knelt, put the carbine down, and said, "I'm going to try to pull you out."

Jobs grabbed Yago under the arms. "When I say three, use your right leg to push against the horse," he said. He ignored the presence of a Blue Meanie, for now. He knew that the second Yago was free the alien would take aim at them both. The Meanie was playing with them. Jobs resented it.

"One. Two. Three!" Jobs pulled. He felt energy surge through his shoulders and arms. Saw Yago's booted right foot pushing against the horse's sweat-slicked back. Heard his own grunts and Yago's.

"Umpf!" Jobs fell back, Yago with him. Yago was free. His left pant leg was torn and the skin Jobs saw beneath the material was scratched and bruised.

"Is it broken? Can you stand?" Jobs demanded.

Yago's breath came in short gasps. "No, I mean, yes, I think I can stand."

Jobs got to his feet, grabbed the carbine, and hauled Yago from the ground. Yago wobbled and put his arm around Jobs's shoulder for balance.

Jobs looked up. The Blue Meanie was still there, only yards away. It raised its front right leg.

"When I say 'run,'" Jobs hissed, "run!"

With a bloodcurdling shriek, Jobs raised the carbine over his head and then hurled it at the Blue Meanie. It clanked off the Meanie's chest.

The ridiculous action took the alien by surprise. The leg lowered and in that instant Jobs yelled, "Run!"

They headed for the corridor leading off the field.

# CHAPTER TWENTY-TWO

## HE KNEW IT WAS GOING TO BE BAD.

"In here!"

The home team's locker room. Open now, though it hadn't been before. Jobs stood panting, holding the door open with his back, shoving the others past him, Yago, 2Face, Miss Blake, Edward, Noyze, and Dr. Cohen.

When everyone was in, Jobs slammed the door shut.

2Face began to push a long bench toward the door.

Everyone grabbed a movable object, heaved it across the tiled floor, jammed it against the door. Laundry bins, trash cans, massage table, more benches.

"We've backed ourselves into a corner!" Miss Blake said. She'd run off into the locker room and was back, panting. "No other way out!"

"What were we going to do, they forced us in here!" Jobs said angrily.

"I'm not saying it was your fault," she retorted.

"Shut up!" 2Face shouted. "Listen!"

Jobs listened and heard nothing at first. Then, a low, persistent sound. Like some sort of drill . . .

"Back away from the door!" he cried.

They did, in a huddle. Just in time to see the center of the door begin to buckle and curdle and disintegrate, then the entire door burn away.

Edward cried out. Yago cursed. A Blue Meanie slowly, confidently drifted into the room, over the piled furniture, and landed on the floor in front of them. On the headpiece of his suit was a red figure. Jobs had never seen that before. It looked vaguely like a Chinese character.

"It's the Muse," Dr. Cohen said, her voice amazingly steady. "One Divine Mountain."

Noyze sighed. "We are in serious trouble now."

"What do we do?" Jobs said.

"Let me try to talk to him."

Noyze stepped forward and wondered, very briefly, how the Muse would react when he discovered that she had understood the Children all along.

Maybe revealing this now was a mistake. Maybe it would get her killed. Maybe it would save them all.

Noyze lifted her hands and began to sign.

Before she'd gotten three words into her plea, the Muse reared on his hind legs. *He's angry*, Noyze thought nervously. "Please, we are not enemies of the Children. But Mother wants us to live. If you kill us you'll only make her more angry with you. I know that's not what you want."

Noyze waited for the Muse to absorb what she'd just told him. For a moment he didn't move. Then, slowly, he dropped down to all fours again.

"We will help you reach Mother," she said, carefully signing. "Together we can help Mother get well."

It was looking good. The Muse . . .

"No!" Noyze shouted. "Please!"

One Divine Mountain had raised his front leg. He was going to kill them.

Jobs had stepped back very, very slowly until he was shoulder to shoulder with Yago.

"Give me the pistol," he whispered. He kept his eyes on Noyze and the Muse.

Yago didn't argue. Jobs took the Remington and very, very slowly moved forward again until he was just behind Noyze.

He knew it was going to be bad. He didn't know how he knew but he knew. When the Muse prepared to fire, Jobs did what he had to do.

In one swift movement he yanked Noyze to the floor and fired.

Screams filled the room, and the sound of people dropping to the floor. One Divine Mountain stumbled but did not fall.

"Stay down!" Jobs yelled. Again he took aim. But before he could pull the trigger, the Muse fired a mini-missile. It went wild, off to the left, nowhere near Jobs and the others. The Muse stumbled again, fell to his knees.

"Look!"

Jobs whirled. Through a thick cloud of black smoke he could see Dr. Cohen, apart from the others, kneeling by a body covered in blood.

"It's Yago," she cried. "He tried to crawl over behind those lockers. He was hit."

"Is he dead?" 2Face asked, getting to her feet.

Jobs watched Dr. Cohen's shoulders heave.

"Yes," she said.

The locker room began to wobble and shimmer. Jobs steadied himself, expecting the entire environment to self-destruct.

He watched as forms blurred and felt the solid floor go soft and heard an odd sort of hush descending . . .

And then it was over. The locker room was back

to what it had been before. Complete with the damage done to one wall by the Muse's missile.

Jobs looked to Miss Blake. "Yago's dead. Shouldn't . . . I thought everything would fall apart and we'd be someplace else. Based on what's happened before."

Miss Blake shook her head. "That's your problem, Jobs. Always thinking."

*I will finish what he has begun.*

*Why do they all fail me? Why?*

*I am betrayed by the strange-eyed one. He promised to destroy the threat. But he failed. The Children are coming closer all the time.*

*They must not reach me. I will not allow it. So I will not let him go, the one who promised to help me.*

*I will finish what he has begun.*

*I will not let him go.*

# CHAPTER TWENTY-THREE

## "IT SHOULD HAVE BEEN ME."

"Easy does it, big guy."

Mo'Steel had Alberto under one arm, supporting him largely with his right shoulder. Kubrick had his father under the other, his left shoulder taking the weight.

It was not going well. They were trying to lower Alberto into one of the pits that were scattered at regular intervals around Mother's basement. Once in there, Alberto could again interface with Mother directly. Maybe, through the fact of his insanity, force her into final deterioration.

Alberto obviously did not want to go. Mo'Steel couldn't blame him. Look at what had happened to the guy the first time he'd gotten up close and personal with Mother. And then, *kah-blam*! Mother had fried his brain.

What did surprise Mo'Steel was that this blabbering, excrement-covered madman was still possessed of enough clarity to know fear and to express resistance.

"Aaaaaaggghhhhh!"

Mo'Steel flinched. The guy had a pair of lungs.

Alberto lunged forward, tried to throw himself out from under the supporting/restraining arms of the boys.

"Papa!" Kubrick shouted. "It'll be okay, I . . . I promise."

Billy was no help, at least with the physical process of lowering a thrashing Alberto into the pit. He might have recovered consciousness, even some degree of normalcy, but the guy was not strong.

"Ahhhhh!"

Mo'Steel flinched again. Then it registered. That cry was human, yeah. But it hadn't come from Alberto.

"There's someone else here!" he hissed to Kubrick.

"Ahhhh! Oh-oh-oh-oh . . ."

Billy cocked his head. "It's coming from over there," he said, pointing generally west.

"Let's go, let's go!" Mo'Steel hefted Alberto to more of a standing position. The fight seemed to have gone out of him.

Mo'Steel and Kubrick half-dragged half-carried Alberto between them, following close behind Billy, avoiding laser sites, checking pits.

Billy found him first.

"In here," Billy said. "It's Yago."

Mo'Steel and Kubrick lowered Alberto to the floor. "Billy," Mo'Steel instructed, "watch him."

"Yago's still hooked up to Mother," Billy said, kneeling by Alberto. The engineer had curled himself into the fetal position and was whimpering.

Yago looked bad. His weird catlike eyes were rolling in his head and his face glistened with sweat. Mo'Steel felt sorry for the guy. He didn't know exactly what Yago had experienced but it had to have been seriously unsettling.

Mo'Steel dropped to his knees, then belly. "Kubrick, grab my ankles."

Mo'Steel was scared. Squeezing the A gland, that's what it was all about. Living life all glandular, no stopping, no saying no.

Yago continued to scream and then yelp like a hurt puppy. He wasn't tied to the chair in any physical way. Unless there were invisible bonds. Didn't matter. Yago was coming out of there.

Mo'Steel reached out for Yago's arm. He was vaguely aware of Billy shouting something.

And then Mo'Steel saw the bones in his outstretched hand and felt a fierce pain race from his head to his feet. He was hot and cold, on fire and freezing. Way, way back in his brain a voice whispered, "My poor, brave boy."

Dimly he felt himself being dragged backward, away from the pit. Yago, still screaming, yelping, screaming. Billy repeating, "It should have been me, it should have been me. . . ."

"No," Kubrick said calmly. "She's angry. She doesn't want to let go. I'll do it. It doesn't matter what happens to me."

*Oh, right,* Mo'Steel thought, on his back, rigid. *Right. Kubrick was the one, no pain and all. . . .*

Mo'Steel heard Yago screaming and Billy mumbling and then a grunt and then a sort of loud sizzle like a million fatty hamburgers being dropped into a million hot frying pans.

Mo'Steel couldn't move his head but he could roll his eyes and he saw Kubrick, his body smoking, carrying Yago.

Mo'Steel wiggled his right index finger. Okay. That worked. Then another finger and then the whole hand and then the toes and feet. Finally he climbed to his feet and staggered over to where Kubrick had laid Yago out. Mo'Steel had a serious dislike of dead things but he sucked it up and pressed his ear against Yago's chest, listened hard. There it was, a heartbeat, faint but steady.

Mo'Steel sat down hard on his butt and looked around at the sorry group. Billy looked stricken and guilty. Alberto was picking at his toes.

Kubrick was staring at his smoking hands.

Mo'Steel put his head on his knees and sighed.

Yago was dead.

Jobs had never liked Yago, but still. He was one of them, one of the ever-dwindling group of survivors. One of the last human beings.

"Someone help me," he said. He knelt by the Muse. "I need to get the suit off him. Maybe we can use it. The other Meanies will find us soon enough."

Noyze knelt at his side. "There's a seam here," she said. "Along the side."

Jobs began to remove the suit. One Divine Mountain looked far less intimidating without his armor. For a moment Jobs felt pity for the hairless, four-legged creature. But he couldn't let sadness overwhelm him like it had so often since they'd come to this ship. Later, maybe, there would be time for grief.

Maybe.

# CHAPTER TWENTY-FOUR

## "MOTHER HAS GONE TO WAR."

Billy was getting something. Something from Mother. What did she want, or not want, Billy to know?

It would come. In the meantime, Billy would wait, keep himself open but also on guard. Mother could not be trusted.

She'd outright attacked Mo'Steel and Kubrick when they'd tried to pull Yago from the pit. What was Yago's significance to her? Why had Mother wanted him so badly at that very moment?

Kubrick seemed to have healed. Mo'Steel was okay, too.

Billy felt tired.

He walked away from the group, from Yago, conscious now but silent, head in his hands; from Mo'Steel, making small jumps in place, always moving; from Kubrick, trying to get his father's shoes back on his feet.

He was hearing something from Mother. Mother had not stopped playing through whatever scenario she had been sucking from Yago's brain. She was angry and she was working on without Yago, but what exactly was happening Billy didn't know. Something bad. And the baby was involved.

An all-too-vivid image tore through Billy, knocking him off his feet. Far, far away. Chechnya, his mother falling, always falling, forever falling to the dusty ground, men shouting, women screaming, a baby seeing it all, recording it all, making memories before full consciousness, understanding nothing, understanding everything.

"That's it," Billy whispered.

"What?" It was Mo'Steel. He stuck out a hand to help Billy to his feet.

"Mother has gone to war. She has to be stopped," Billy said, holding Mo'Steel's eyes, willing him to understand. "We *have* to stop her."

Mo'Steel continued to look at Billy with an expression of honest puzzlement. Then, "Oh. You really think it's necessary?"

Billy nodded. "I do."

"Right. I think Yago can help us now."

"I'll help, too," Billy insisted.

Mo'Steel grinned, though the grin was a bit shaky. "Okay, I'll talk to Kubrick and Yago."

Billy waited. Then he heard his name called softly and he joined the others.

"Me and Kubrick, his arms. Yago and Billy, his legs. Be as gentle as you can, but don't let go."

Billy glanced at the others. No one looked happy. But no one was protesting, either. Least of all poor Alberto, who seemed to be on the verge of sleep, his head resting on his chest, legs splayed out before him.

Billy took hold of Alberto's left foot.

"On the count of three."

Jobs hoped the suit's controls were technological, something he could figure out. If the suit worked by some sort of mind-speak or directed thought, he would be helpless.

"I won't be able to wear it," he said to Noyze, peering inside. "But maybe I can fire the fléchette gun or the mini-missiles."

Jobs spotted a series of tiny buttons inside the right tentacle.

"I think this . . ."

Someone screamed.

Jobs fell back on his butt, still holding the suit.

Three Blue Meanies were crowding the doorway.

One by one, they entered the room. The one closest to Jobs looked in his direction. Jobs knew he recognized the Muse's special suit.

It was now or never.

The Blue Meanie closest took aim at Jobs.

Jobs reached in and pressed one of the tiny buttons.

"Whoa!" Noyze fell back in surprise.

"Get down!" Jobs shouted, though the kickback had already thrown him flat on his back.

He hadn't fired the mini-missiles at all. Instead he'd fired the suit's rockets and now it was shooting wildly around the locker room like a punctured balloon.

Jobs turned on his stomach and covered his head with his hands. He hoped the others were doing the same.

And then, with a tremendous crash, the suit hit a wall of lockers and sputtered to the floor. Jobs raised his head. The Blue Meanies had advanced.

"No!" Noyze scrambled to her feet and stood, panting, between Jobs and the Meanies.

"Noyze!" It was Dr. Cohen.

Jobs slowly got to his feet. He watched as Noyze began to sign to the three Meanies. Her hands were a blur in the air and she spoke as rapidly.

"Listen to me, please! Didn't these people come here willingly to warn you of Mother's army? Spare our lives and we'll do everything we can to help you. . . ."

One of the Meanies signed back. Noyze's hands dropped.

"What did he say?" Jobs asked.

Noyze gave an odd little laugh. "He said, 'Prepare to be destroyed.' "

*What is this one doing here? He was useless to me before. He can only be useless to me again.*

*I did not set out to cause such damage. I was more gentle with the angry, strange-eyed one, wasn't I? I did not mean any harm.*

*So, I will listen to him this time. I will see what he has to offer. I sensed an intelligence when first we met. Perhaps there is still something he has to share.*

*So, let us begin.*

# CHAPTER TWENTY-FIVE

## "THAT BABY IS NOT HUMAN."

*So, that's it,* Jobs thought. *Well, I can't say it's been dull.*

And then . . . in the doorway . . .

"Twelve Hallowed Stones!" Noyze cried.

For some reason the alien was standing on his hind legs, one front leg held awkwardly behind him.

"Please," Noyze said, "we beg you to spare our lives. I know you can understand me. Please help us."

Jobs waited, tense.

Without warning, Twelve Hallowed Stones pulled a repeating rifle from behind his back and opened fire on the other Meanies.

It was not what Jobs had expected.

"No!" he heard Noyze cry. "I didn't mean . . ."

Twelve Hallowed Stones stepped over the body of the Muse.

And that's when Jobs saw the baby. Riding on the

arched back of Twelve Hallowed Stones's suit. Its toothy grin wide, blank eyes watering, chubby hands clasped.

"What is that?!" Dr. Cohen shrieked.

"It's all right," Jobs said, though he was far from sure that was true. "It's one of the survivors, from the *Mayflower*. It was born during the mother's hibernation."

"It's not Twelve Hallowed Stones in the suit," Miss Blake said.

"Tamara," 2Face guessed.

The baby giggled wildly. Dr. Cohen's expression was a mix of horror and curiosity.

Tamara leaned down and tore the suit off one of the dead Meanies.

Then Tamara lowered herself to the floor and helped slide the baby off her back. She placed the baby near the body.

"What is she doing?" Dr. Cohen whispered.

Silently the group watched as the baby's skin began to darken, then flush red. The red became brighter and extended beyond the baby's body, like a hellish halo.

"It looks radioactive," Miss Blake said softly.

And then the glow . . . It seemed to be dissolving the body of the Meanie.

By the end the Blue Meanie was gone, no trace. And the baby was beginning to — change.

"What's it doing?" Edward asked. He sounded scared, but fascinated, too.

"I don't know," Jobs said.

The baby's form was expanding. Its skin faded until it was translucent. All but for the skin of its now cone-shaped head. That was opaque and quivering. When the transformation was complete, the thing had no discernable limbs.

"Shipwright," Jobs said. Not exactly the same as Mother's form back at the diner. But close enough.

"That baby is not human," Dr. Cohen said. Her voice shook.

"You think?" 2Face asked no one in particular.

In the time it took to blink, the baby was once again a toddler-sized infant with a full set of pointy white teeth and empty eye sockets.

And it was laughing. It turned its head to Jobs and Jobs knew that somehow the baby was watching him.

And there was nothing he could do about it.

And then the locker room shook and the walls dissolved and Jobs found himself in a place that was no particular place but the entire stadium at once. And the entire stadium was destructing.

The environment was dying. The node was being destroyed. Jobs wondered if the baby had done it and then realized it didn't matter.

Jobs could see sky above and ground below. He was vaguely aware of the others nearby but also far, far away. He tried to lift his arm to reach for someone, anyone, but his arm was too, too heavy.

So Jobs just watched the show.

Huge pieces of the stadium separated from the whole, like all along the stadium had been a massive, three-dimensional jigsaw puzzle. The pieces, each one a vast, unique, multiedged shape, flew through the air in that fast-then-slow-then-fast pattern that Jobs had seen back at the exploding diner.

It was mesmerizing.

Individual units twisted and whirled through the air like the debris of a tornado.

"Like *The Wizard of Oz*." Miss Blake. Suddenly, she was next to Jobs. The tatters of her dress lifted as if on a gentle breeze and floated around her legs. "It's almost lovely."

Jobs reached for Miss Blake's hand and it was there, reaching for his.

Something else was happening.

The scent of lemon was overpowering and wonderful, fresh lemon. And fresh baked bread, too, an unbelievable smell that made Jobs almost fall to his knees. He'd been indifferent to food back on Earth but now, now there was passion.

And strains of music, lovely, soaring melodies, a voice singing words Jobs could not understand but which spoke to him anyway, spoke to the poet in him.

"Opera," Miss Blake whispered. "Puccini."

Jobs listened and tears leaked down his cheeks. He'd always thought he didn't like this sort of music. But this, this . . . Who was doing this? This wasn't only Mother now, so who?

Suddenly, Jobs, 2Face, Miss Blake, Edward, Noyze, Dr. Cohen were all running, running, but where could they go in a landscape that was shifting beneath their feet?

They were falling, falling, falling, whipped in ever-tightening circles, down, down, down. . . .

Until they were dumped down on the floor of Mother's hull. Not only those who had been with Jobs but the others, too. Mrs. Gonzalez. Burroway. T.R. Tate, Roger Dodger, D-Caf, and Anamull. Even Tamara and the baby.

Someone pulled Jobs to his feet.

"Welcome to my world, Duck."

It was Mo'Steel. And Yago. That was a surprise. And there was Alberto, writhing and babbling in a big chair set in a pit. Next to him stood Billy and Kubrick.

Jobs turned back to Mo'Steel. "Sorry we're late."

# CHAPTER TWENTY-SIX

## "IT'S GETTING CLOSER!"

Something made Mo'Steel look up. He was glad he did.

"Move, move, move!" he shouted.

It was the Washington Monument. And it was spiraling slowly down through the sky above, though there shouldn't be a sky, just a ceiling. And the needlelike structure shouldn't be falling point down, so slowly and aimed right for Alberto.

They had maybe a minute. Who knew when Mother would decide to give the massive lance a shove. Mo'Steel jumped down into the pit with Kubrick and Billy. He was aware of the others scattering.

"Watch the lasers!" he shouted.

Suddenly, Alberto's eyes pulled open wide and a trembling smile came to his lips. For the first time in a while he began to form words. His voice was thick and drooly, like the victim of a stroke.

"What is he saying?!" Kubrick demanded.

Billy shook his head.

"It's Latin."

Violet, crouched at the edge of the pit.

*"Mors omnibus communes."*

"Papa!" Kubrick cried.

"Thanks, Miss Blake," Mo'Steel said. "But you'd better step away."

"It's getting closer!" That was Olga. "Romeo, get out of there!"

Mo'Steel shot a glance upward. Oh, yeah. Heading straight for Alberto.

Kubrick grabbed his father's arms and pulled.

"He's stuck!" he wailed. "Help me!"

Mo'Steel grabbed, too. No shock this time. He put his back into it but it was like Alberto was welded to the chair.

"I don't think he wants out," Mo'Steel said.

Alberto lifted his eyes and smiled again.

And then it happened. The monument accelerated and spun faster and faster and Mo'Steel said, "Billy! Now!"

Mo'Steel saw Billy close his eyes and then he

and Billy and Kubrick were ascending from the pit, Kubrick's green eyes on his father. Billy lifted them up and away and just as they rose out of harm's way, the monument rocketed into the pit.

It was a rush of air bigger than the one that had sent them all tumbling back when the Blue Meanies had first invaded.

Violet was thrown to her knees. She squinted against the wind. It felt like her hair would be whipped from her skull, her skin from her body. She knew the air pressure was dropping, could feel it in her ears, behind her eyes.

The monument had breached the hull. They were going to explode, freeze, suffocate. Their bodies, what was left of them, would hang around in space, so much trash.

*It can't possibly get any worse,* Violet thought and knew it probably would.

From the shadows of the basement came a detail of Blue Meanies. They ignored Violet and the other Remnants grasping tight to one another and raced toward the pit where Alberto had lost his fight.

"What are they doing?" Poor Kubrick. Where was he?

"They want to repair the breach." Noyze, gasping.

Violet jerked.

"Those were missiles! They're trying to kill us!"

"No." Jobs. "We're incidental to them. The Meanies just want to save Mother."

Jobs, always explaining.

"Mother's not healing herself," someone said.

"Maybe she's depressed."

Now, who was that? Violet's head landed on the floor. Her lungs were burning. If only . . .

The floor was soft and damp and sandy. It was a nice place to sleep.

If only Jobs would stop telling her to wake up.

It was a little drier than the default environment they'd been thrown into after node thirty-one had been destroyed. But the water, only a few feet in some places, was still lukewarm and copper-colored. This was more of a swamp, less of an ocean dotted with islands.

In the twilight distance Jobs saw a small herd of the salmon-colored blimplike creatures hovering over a distant island. The skittish palm trees were there, too, swaying and trembling with every hint of a breeze. Best of all, no Riders in sight.

Yet.

Slowly, like pale ghosts of themselves, people wandered over to one another. Jobs couldn't imagine what they were saying. Nice day. Fancy meeting you here. Hey, wahoo, we're still alive. Everyone looked bedraggled and thin and very, very tired.

Miss Blake seemed okay. She'd passed out back in the basement and when, suddenly, they'd found themselves in this default environment, Mo'Steel had scooped her up and hurried along with the others. Away from the Blue Meanies still frantically trying to repair Mother's hull.

"I'm not getting anything from Mother," Billy said abruptly. "The power node must be dead."

"Where do you think she is?" Jobs asked.

"I don't know," Billy said worriedly. "Maybe she finally crashed. Went totally crazy. Maybe she's still alive and functioning in other areas of the ship. I can't tell."

"Do you miss her?" Mo'Steel asked.

"Yes," Billy admitted. "She's kind of a friend."

Mo'Steel grinned. "I have a feeling we haven't seen the last of her, 'migo."

*We'll find her at the bridge,* Jobs thought. *We have to.*

# CHAPTER TWENTY-SEVEN

## "IT'S TIME TO CHOOSE."

They were a mess.

No one was in charge and no one wanted to be. Not even Yago, her main nemesis, who had been badly shaken up by his interface with Mother. So far 2Face hadn't heard him say a word to anyone. Though she had noticed his lips moving and his eyes focused on the middle distance, like a street person talking to some invisible companion.

The other kids were out. Dr. Cohen and Olga Gonzalez were nice but not tough enough.

2Face was worried. Things had gone from bad to worse. They needed a direction, something.

Most of all, they needed to get far away from Tamara and the baby.

2Face was scared but more than that, she wanted to be free.

Tamara and the baby, perched on her hip, were

standing in the center of the ragged circle of survivors.

2Face broke through.

"What do you want?" she demanded loudly. She was aware of people watching, listening.

Tamara said nothing, which 2Face knew meant the baby didn't want her to respond.

"This is one of them," 2Face said, pointing. "The baby is a Shipwright. It's true, isn't it?" she challenged.

The baby only giggled, its small white teeth bared in a frightening grin.

2Face was freaked out but not enough to keep her mouth shut. "You don't belong with us," she said. "Go away and leave us alone."

Tamara laughed. "If the baby is what you say it is, shouldn't you be treating it with more respect?"

"No," 2Face said strongly. "We didn't ask to be here. The baby — the Shipwright — is the violator. It's already made *you* into a toy," she said, nodding to Tamara. "I don't know what exactly it wants, but I do know it's not interested in helping us."

"You talk as though you can defy the baby," Tamara shot back.

"I can't," 2Face admitted. "But Billy can, can't he?"

This time, the baby didn't smile. Tamara said nothing but stared, and the baby stared through her, at Billy. And Billy, knowing he was being watched, looked up and stared back.

2Face watched the contest of wills. Yes, both Billy and the baby were powerful. Maybe neither knew just how powerful. Maybe neither was willing to find out just yet.

"It's time to choose," 2Face said loudly. It was a risk, but she was taking it. She looked at Jobs and Violet. "We're leaving. You're with us or you're with Tamara and the Shipwright."

The look that flitted across Tamara's face surprised 2Face. Maybe she'd imagined it — the look had come and gone so quickly. It was a look of admiration. Now it was replaced by one of hardness.

"Yes, certainly, all of you, choose your sides," Tamara said, voice menacing. "But keep this in mind as you decide where to bestow your loyalty: The baby knows where the bridge is located. The baby knows where Mother is to be found. And no one else here does. No one."

2Face clutched her hands into fists at her sides. She didn't need to be reminded of just how little she knew.

Tamara went on, "This ship can be Earth. The Earth you left so unfortunately. Imagine: You can all go home again. The baby can make that happen."

Suddenly, Yago was standing next to 2Face. "What do you mean?" he said. They were the first words he'd spoken in a long time.

"The baby can re-create your favorite, dearly loved Earth environments right here on this ship. The baby can reconfigure Mother to do that, and only the baby."

No. 2Face felt suddenly, horribly defeated. The baby's offer was too much to resist.

Then, a thought occurred to 2Face. The baby needed them, didn't it? Why else would it be trying to convince the humans to follow it? The baby needed them. But why?

And why only now was the baby making this outrageous offer? What did the timing mean?

"It is how it should be," Yago declared. 2Face shot him a questioning look. He sounded like he was reading from an official document. His eyes were still focused on something, nothing, out there. "Those who understand will join me and follow."

Yago walked slowly over to Tamara and the baby. D-Caf scurried to his side, though 2Face saw the kid shoot his own curious glances up at Yago.

"Who else shall be one of the Chosen?" Yago intoned.

It came down to this. 2Face, the silently acknowledged leader. 2Face and Jobs and, of course, where there was Jobs there was Mo'Steel. And Edward. And where there was Jobs there was also Violet, a fact that annoyed 2Face, though she didn't know why.

Noyze and Dr. Cohen, they'd teamed up early. Kubrick, because he and Mo'Steel had seen stuff together. And because everyone had heard Burroway call Kubrick obscene. Kubrick wouldn't be safe with that bunch. Finally, Olga, because she was Mo'Steel's mother.

The others — Yago, Tate, Roger Dodger, and D-Caf, and the other adults, T.R., Burroway — went off with Tamara and the baby/Shipwright. Yago, clearly, had lost it. Who could guess at his motive? The others thought they were going home.

Maybe they were, 2Face thought. Maybe now she and Jobs and the others were the true exiles.

2Face had spent every waking moment on this ship fighting against the panicky prejudice of those who'd gone off with Yago. She'd literally fought for her life, done things she knew were wrong — like trying to sacrifice Wylson Lefkowitz-Blake to the baby. All to avoid being labeled the outsider. To avoid becoming the scapegoat.

But what had she done this time? What exactly had she accomplished by declaring independence from the baby and urging others to do the same?

"No," 2Face told herself. "Don't do this." She'd made her choice and now was not the time to second-guess.

Purposefully, as if she had a plan, 2Face led her band off into the island's swamps. She walked out front, alone.

After a while someone joined her. Jobs.

They walked on in silence for a bit. Then Jobs said quietly, "Where are we going?"

2Face almost smiled. "I have absolutely no idea."

K.A. APPLEGATE

# REMNANTS™

7

## Isolation

"RIDERS!"

Billy was not asleep. He was aware of the others' conversation. More aware of it than they could ever be.

His ears heard their words. He sensed feelings that rose, fell, shifted, and mixed like notes in a complicated piece of music. Nine minds harmonizing.

Mo'Steel's excitement. 2Face's smug satisfaction with finally being in charge. Jobs's curiosity. Dr. Cohen's loneliness for her husband. 2Face's worry. Kubrick's tender feelings toward 2Face. 2Face's indifference toward Kubrick. Kubrick's fury with 2Face's indifference. Edward's cozy, sleepy response to seeing his mother's face in a dream.

Some of the emotions came and went almost faster than Billy could register them. Others — like Olga's affection for her son — never wavered.

Finally Billy closed his mind to the cacophony. He spun the dial and tried to tune into what else was happening on the ship.

There.

Mother. She was weak, deteriorating fast. Only an echo of what she had been. But still alive. Still dangerous. She was directing thousands of Squids all over the ship, preparing them to go into battle to protect her.

Again Billy spun the dial.

There.

Far away, like fireworks in the next town, the minds of the other Remnants. They were chiming the same high notes over and over. Fear. Indecision. Moral outrage. Anger.

Billy sat up. "Something is happening to the others. They're —" Billy hesitated, unsure of what adjective to choose when so many fit.

Then —

The same panicked high notes. Much clearer, closer. Coming from Mo'Steel and Kubrick.

"Riders!" Mo'Steel shouted. "There has to be thirty of them, coming this way!"

Panic, indecision, fear. The emotions swarming around him made Billy dizzy, nauseous.

"Run!" 2Face ordered.

From the Riders came a chorus of shrieks like the brakes of a runaway train. Their battle cry.

Jobs searching through a field. Unable to find his younger brother because his skin had turned straw-colored and blended into the grass. "Edward! Edward, where are you?"

Edward sitting up with a confused, sleepy expression. Jobs pulling him to his feet, urging him forward.

They were running. Billy with 2Face, Jobs, Edward, Kubrick, and Mo'Steel ahead of him and the others behind. Running the same direction they'd been heading. Only now the Riders were chasing them.

Down the hill. Slipping, sliding, grass slapping them in the face, unable to see where their feet were landing. Edward fell and rolled until Mo'Steel grabbed him and yanked him up. The bottom of the hill. Water. They splashed through and started up the hill on the other side.

Pointless, futile. They were inchworms trying to outrun greyhounds. The Riders on their hover-boards are closing fast, yelling their bloodthirsty cry.

Billy heard the others' thoughts, jumbled together like a panic variety pack. Horrifying images of death. Spears piercing flesh. A bloodied head held aloft, eyes staring. A frantic Rider mouth disgorging a human skull.

The worst were Noyze and Dr. Cohen. They'd never seen Riders and what they imagined was even worse than reality — floods of blood, enormous mouths with rows of teeth, human bodies roasted over fires like chickens on a rotisserie.

Billy couldn't block the other's minds out. Couldn't concentrate on blocking them and run at the same time. They were too persistent, too panicked.

Noyze cried out. Billy shot a look toward the sound. He saw her topple backward, arms flung out, mouth open. She fell and disappeared into the tall grass.

"Someone help!" Dr. Cohen shouted.

Then the Riders were on them, the grass shushing aside to reveal a swarm of hoverboards, each one topped by a warrior with his spear at the ready. The Riders' eating mouths gnashed. They shrieked so loudly that Billy covered his ears. What could the humans do? They were defenseless. The Riders were closing in. Ten feet. Five!

"Get down!" 2Face bellowed. "Hide in the grass."

Billy dropped onto his hands and knees and then onto his belly. His face hit the dirt. He tasted gritty soil on his tongue.

A crash off to his right. The grass waved and Violet rolled into view. They stared at each other, eyes wild, breathing deeply, not daring to talk. Billy was happy it was Violet. Happy that the last thing he would see was her pretty face.

Riders! Two, seven, ten hoverboards rushing at them, blocking out the sky and then —

They were past!

Past. And Billy was still alive. He blinked. Violet stared, too shocked to move.

Billy stood up. Shaky, dirty, confused. He offered Violet a hand. She got up, brushed the dirt and grass off her dress. Billy turned 360 degrees and saw the heads of his friends appearing in the tall grass around him.

The Riders had already crested the next hill. Their cries were fading into the distance. Violet and Billy began to walk toward 2Face, toward where all of the others were gathering.

Dr. Cohen had a wide, amazed smile. She gave Noyze a sideways hug.

2Face was counting heads like a teacher on a field trip. "Everyone is here," she said briskly.

"You okay?" Olga asked Mo'Steel.

"Fine, Mom. You?" Mo'Steel asked.

"A few scrapes and scratches," Olga said. "Nothing serious."

"Why didn't they wipe us out?" Edward asked.

Jobs shook his head. "Good question."

"They sure seemed to be in a hurry," Violet said.

"Maybe the fight has already started," Jobs said.

"Let's just say we were lucky and leave it at that. We've got to reach the bridge. Time to move." 2Face.

"The others," Billy said. "Tate. Yago. Something is happening to them. Something bad."

Jobs, Violet, and Mo'Steel exchanged looks.

"Can we help them?" Noyze asked.

Billy shrugged. "I — I'm not sure where they are."

One by one, the others turned to 2Face. Waited for her to decide.

"Time to move," she said.

## "I GET THE MESSAGE."

The Riders were preparing for battle. Half a dozen Chiefs, plus Tamara with the Baby on her back, crouched together in a circle. They drew in the peaty soil with sticks, arguing in their strange clicking language. Generals planning strategy.

The remaining Riders — the ones Tate thought of as the troops — seemed to be killing time. They fished in the copper-colored sea, built fires, sharpened spears and boomerangs, and drank from small green flasks they removed from their bandoleers.

Tate sat against a tree, eating a piece of fish. One of the Riders had given the little group of humans a crude bowl full of the charred eel-like creatures. The fish was surprisingly delicious, flavored with the smoke from the fire. All Tate could wish for was some salt and pepper. And maybe a plate, a napkin, and a fork and spoon.

"Watch out for the bones," Roger Dodger said. He was nearby, leaning against another one of the endless trees.

T.R. and Burroway were farther off, poking a fire they'd built, seemingly lost in their thoughts or regrets. Tate had no desire to join them. Yago was talking quietly and urgently to Anamull and D-Caf. The boys both looked anxious to escape.

"Lots of little bones," Roger Dodger warned her.

"I'll be careful." The others were ignoring Roger Dodger, so Tate had encouraged him to sit with her. He wasn't a bad kid.

"My dad got a trout bone caught in his throat once," Roger Dodger said, starting to giggle. "We were camping. The closest hospital was about fifty miles away and Dad gagged and gagged and finally threw up all over the car."

Tate smiled. "Was he okay?"

"Yeah." Roger Dodger sobered up. "But it doesn't really matter too much now, does it?"

Tate didn't say anything. She wondered what

Roger Dodger had been like back on Earth. Probably just a kid, playing with his video games and doing homework. Thinking about how much his life had changed made Tate sad.

The Remnants tended to think of themselves as lucky. After all, they were the ones who survived. But maybe they'd gotten that backwards. Maybe Roger Dodger was right and the lucky ones were the ones who had perished before humans ever heard of the Rock.

Tate watched as Tamara and the Baby separated from the ever-growing group of Riders and approached T.R. and Burroway's fire. Tamara put the Baby down and helped herself to some of the food. The men moved away silently as Tamara crouched down and began to eat. Exactly the chance Tate had been waiting for.

"I'll be back," Tate told Roger Dodger. She stood up and approached the fire. She picked up a piece of fish and then gave Tamara a tentative smile. "Not bad, huh?"

Tamara's face was like stone. Her eyes showed no warmth, no recognition, no humanity. She could have been a machine.

The Baby reacted by baring its pointy little white

teeth at Tate. It crawled between Tamara and Tate and glared in Tate's direction.

"I get the message," Tate said coldly to the Baby. Her stomach was twisting with fear, but she refused to show it. Nobody bullied her. Nobody.

She longed to put a hand on Tamara's shoulder, to let her know she wasn't alone. But that wasn't happening — not with the Baby standing guard.

Reluctantly, Tate retreated to her spot under the trees. Roger Dodger had dozed off, still sitting up.

Tate flashed back on the one moment she'd seen pure humanity shining from Tamara's eyes: When the Baby had transformed into a Shipwright. Then, when the Baby was strong enough to move and speak for itself, the connection with Tamara had been broken. For those brief moments, Tamara had seemed lost. Tate regretted not approaching her then, not trying to convince her to resist the Baby's control.

So she had missed one opportunity. That didn't mean she could give up. She just had to try again.

But when?

The answer was obvious: When the Baby consumed another Blue Meanie. It looked as if the Baby was going to have plenty of opportunities, considering the enormous ranks of Riders who were about to declare war on the Meanies.

War.

Tate wasn't thrilled with the idea of turning the Meanies into enemies. The humans' survival seemed precarious enough already. Why antagonize a group of aliens that possessed superior firepower?

She wondered if the Meanies already thought of them as enemies. Mother had forced the humans to attack the Meanies. The battle had been ridiculous — with Yago and his toadies riding in on horseback and the rest of them dressed up like extras in a Civil War regiment. The humans had been completely out-gunned. They were lucky the Meanies hadn't turned it into a total massacre.

And then there was Billy.

Billy.

Could it be that the Baby was interested in Billy?

Or scared of him?

Tate felt lightning-struck. Maybe she was wrong about the Baby wanting to use Billy or being scared of him. But, even if she was wrong, Billy was the strongest person among them and the most able to help them.

He should know what the Baby was up to.

Tate sat up on her heels, full of energy but unsure of exactly what to do.

First things first. If she was right about the Baby,

she had to warn Billy and the others about what was going on. Maybe, if she could find the others quickly, she could be back before the battle began, before the Baby could absorb any more Meanies.

Tate crawled over to Roger Dodger and shook his shoulder. "Wake up," she whispered.

Roger Dodger opened his eyes, silently alert.

"I'm going to go look for the others," Tate told him as quietly as possible. "We need to warn them about Tamara and the Riders."

Roger Dodger bit his lip. "Can I come?"

Tate nodded and got up. "Follow me. Quietly." She turned toward the woods and instantly noticed a figure among the trees — not five feet away.

D-Caf.

And she could tell from his expression that he had heard everything.

Light-Years From Home...And On Their Own
REMNANTS
THE MAYFLOWER PROJECT
K.A. APPLEGATE
REMNANTS
DESTINATION UNKNOWN
REMNANTS
K.A. Applegate
K.A. APPLEGATE
REMNANTS
THEM
K.A. APPLEGATE
REMNANTS
NOWHERE LAND
K.A. APPLEGATE
REMNANTS
MUTATION
K.A. APPLEGATE
REMNANTS
NOT FINAL ART
BREAKDOWN
BGA 0-590-87997-9 Remnants #1: The Mayflower Project $4.99 US
BGA 0-590-88074-8 Remnants #2: Destination Unknown $4.99 US
BGA 0-590-88078-0 Remnants #3: Them $4.99 US
BGA 0-590-88193-0 Remnants #4: Nowhere Land $4.99 US
BGA 0-590-88194-9 Remnants #5: Mutation $4.99 US
BGA 0-590-88195-7 Remnants #6: Breakdown $4.99 US
Available wherever you buy books, or use this order form.
Scholastic Inc., P.O. Box 7502, Jefferson City, MO 65102
Please send me the books I have checked above. I am enclosing $___________ (please add $2.00 to cover shipping and handling). Send check or money order—no cash or C.O.D.s please.
Name__________ Birth date__________
Address__________
City__________ State/Zip__________
Please allow four to six weeks for delivery. Offer good in U.S.A. only. Sorry, mail orders are not available to residents of Canada. Prices subject to change.
Continue the exciting journey on-line at www.scholastic.com/remnants
SCHOLASTIC
REM502